Behind Church Doors

A Novel

Sylvia Brown-Roberts

iUniverse, Inc.

New York   Bloomington

iUniverse books may be ordered through booksellers or by contacting:

iUniverse
1663 Liberty Drive
Bloomington, IN 47403
www.iuniverse.com
1-800-Authors (1-800-288-4677)

Because of the dynamic nature of the Internet, any Web addresses or links contained in this
book may have changed since publication and may no longer be valid. The views expressed
in this work are solely those of the author and do not necessarily reflect the views of the
publisher, and the publisher hereby disclaims any responsibility for them.

ISBN: 978-1-4401-8970-8 (sc)
ISBN: 978-1-4401-8968-5 (hc)
ISBN: 978-1-4401-8969-2 (ebook)

Printed in the United States of America

iUniverse rev. date: 1/4/2009

Acknowledgements

I am ever thankful to God for His mercy and His grace. I am thankful for the Bible, His inspired word.

Many people have been blessings to me in life and certainly throughout the writing of this book. I thank God for them all.

Thank you, Ellis J. Crumb. The hymn titles are from *Sacred Selections For The Church*, Compiled and Edited by Ellis J. Crumb, Copyright 1956, 1959, 1960, Sacred Selections, Kendallville, Indiana. Used by permission.

Thank you to my parents, Mary Brown and the late Fitzhugh Brown. You raised me and my siblings (Alfred, Peggy, Michael, Raymond) in a loving Christian household. There is no greater gift parents can give their children. I truly love and appreciate my family.

I have many sister friends, but only one sister by birth. Thank you, Peggy Brown. For many years you prompted me with the words, "Birth that book, already!" You have always been my biggest cheerleader and fan.

Thank you, Pamela D. Washington. You are the sister I call my manager and chief resource person.

Thank you, Evelyn Jones Busby. I will always appreciate your support, professionalism, and willing spirit, my sister.

Thank you to the many faithful ministers of God and the Bible teachers whose sermons and lessons I have taken in for most of my life.

Thank you to all my brothers and sisters in Christ.

Thank you to my husband Anthony, who understands that I need to write.

Thank you to my readers. I appreciate your support.

Chapter 1   Best Friends Forever

Nikolis McQuaige is the name on my birth certificate, but I prefer to be called NikkiMac. I didn't give myself that nickname; my sister friend Jacee gave it to me. One day long ago, she and I were both "cuttin' the fool," as our old southern relatives say. Good-natured ribbing has been our pattern since the start of this friendship.

"Girl, I've been meaning to ask you this for the longest time. Nikolis sounds like a boy's name. How did your parents come up with that first name for you?" We were walking over the Southard Street Bridge on our way home from Junior High School Number One.

"Jacee, you know that my father's first name is Nickson and my mother's first name is Alice. Being the creative people they are, they sort of combined the two and came up with Nikolis. Mom says that they can hear the flavor of both of their names when they say mine. I like that. But excuse you, Missy. You truly don't have room to talk, because your first and middle names are unusual names also, Jacee Fontinetta. You sound like a country cousin."

"Oh no you didn't just crack on me like that, Nikolis McQuaige!" We laughed heartily, acting silly like the two twelve-year-old girls we were.

"But Nikolis, how many Black folks in Trenton do you know with McQuaige as a last name? As a matter of fact, how many Black folks in this country have a Scottish surname? Tell you what; I'm going to call you NikkiMac. I think that's a really cool nickname for you; it's jazzy."

I remember thinking; Jacee has forgotten the whole American slavery experience. How does she think most Black folks in America got their last names? Where does she think Jackson, her last name, came from? It certainly didn't come from Africa!

One of the things I loved about her from the start was her energetic, effervescent personality. I quickly found out that she often talked off the top of her head, so I dutifully nailed her down to facts. This never seemed to bother her, though.

We found each other when we were both nine years old and in the fourth grade at Woodrow Wilson Elementary School in Trenton, New Jersey. Jacee and her family moved from North Carolina to our east Trenton neighborhood.

"Class, we have a new student named Jacee. She just moved to Trenton from North Carolina." Miss Major, our teacher, waited for us to get quiet and pay attention.

"Let's all politely greet Jacee."

I looked up from my math assignment and stared into the large, hazel brown eyes of a skinny, bowlegged, bushy-haired girl with skin the color of milk chocolate. She blinked nervously and squeezed out a crooked smile as we all chanted on cue, "Hello Jacee. Welcome to our class."

"Thank you. It's nice to meet you all. I'm Jacee Fontinetta Jackson." She twisted a section of her afro with her fingers and slowly looked at all of us.

I don't know why, but I got up from my seat and approached her. "There's an empty seat next to mine because Claretha transferred to Grant School. You can be my new desk partner, Jacee. Is that okay with you, Miss Major?"

"That's fine, Nikolis. You can help Jacee get accustomed to our class and school routines."

That was the beginning of the BFF (Best Friends Forever) life of Nikolis McQuaige and Jacee Fontinetta Jackson. Later that day, Jacee and I discovered that we lived around the corner from each other. She lived on Hart Avenue, and I lived on Poplar Street. There was an alley behind our streets, where all the neighborhood children played many games of *Hide and Seek; Hide and Go Get It; One, Two, Three, Red Light*, and anything else that allowed us to run and holler. At dusk, when the streetlights came on, we all knew it was curfew, so we'd head to our houses for the night. From my bedroom window at the rear of my house, I could see Jacee's back bedroom window. Many nights we'd blink our bedroom lights, signaling to each other with codes we created.

We were graduated from Woodrow Wilson Elementary School and attended Junior High School Number One from the seventh through ninth grade. Our junior and senior high school classmates called us

"The Twins," but not because we looked alike. Jacee's dark brown skin contrasted with my buttery skin tone. Her fluffy wild afro framed a heart-shaped face that was punctuated with her incredible hazel eyes. Jacee's short, petite frame was in perfect proportion. She resembled a delicate doll, but she was feisty and full of energy. I was considered a redbone because of my light complexion and red hair. My freckles and heavy eyebrows added a curiosity to my face. More handsome than pretty, I wore my hair long and straight, with short bangs. I was always fuller in body and taller than Jacee. Though we were physically different, the twins' moniker stuck because we were inseparable.

After high school, we attended and were graduated from Rutgers University. True to our twins' behavior, we both majored in Urban Teacher Education. Following graduation, we gained employment as teachers in the Trenton Public School system. This is where we had to separate. Even though we sought to work in the same elementary school, it didn't happen. I was assigned to a school in west Trenton and Jacee to a school in east Trenton. Yet, we still pursue our passion to educate urban children. I often smile when I think about the fact that we have been together since elementary school.

Now I am forty years old, and like most of my sisters in America, I struggle to keep my weight down. I carry 150 pounds on a 5 foot 7 inch curvy frame. The cool thing is that my figure is fairly proportionate: 38 inch bust, 32 inch waist, 38 inch hips. I have big legs and a booty that draws attention. I used to like that attention when I was in my twenties, fingerpoppin' at the club. Jacee and NikkiMac used to show out on the dance floor. The guys loved it.

"Go on, girl, with all that junk in your trunk!"

"Shake it, but don't break it, Pretty Mama!"

"Work your body, work your body. Make sure you don't hurt nobody!"

Back in the day, I loved hearing men in the club say these things to me. I'd reward my admirers with an extra wiggle, a wink, and a sexy smile. You couldn't tell me a thing back in those high-spirited, party-minded days; but now I'm glad they're behind me. At age thirty, even though I was enjoying it less, I was still hanging out on the weekends. Most of the time, Jacee was right there with me. I think it was more that she wanted to be wherever I was than that she wanted to be at the club. Fortunately, thanks to an experience with both a devil and an older Christian man, I had what I guess one would call an epiphany.

"Enough," I thought. "Why am I getting all dressed up to sit at a club trying to see how many drinks I can get for free, knowing that I'm not giving up any booty at the end of the night? Why spend two to four hours with people who don't know the real me? Why seek attention from folks who don't know I have a working brain? Why tease married men? I've been there, done that, and I'm not proud of it. What am I doing to myself? What is my life's purpose? Why did God put me on this earth?" It dawned on me that I was spending a lot of time with folks who were going in a different direction than the way I wanted to go. I was hanging out as a diversion from taking a serious look at my personal life.

I'll never forget my last night of partying at the club.

Chapter 2   From Darkness to Light

"See you all later," I called to my acquaintances, Leisha and Nicole, at Club Taste. The club was my hangout place on Friday and Saturday nights. Located on Olden Avenue, it was just over the bridge, not far from my house. Club Taste was nestled into a corner of the Captain's Plaza Shopping Center. I was partying without Jacee because she had to work at her part-time job. Alex Carson, my guy pal, had been partying with me earlier, but he had to leave for another engagement.

"Goodnight, NikkiMac. Drive safely." Leisha and Nicole raised their glasses of gin and tonic.

"I'll check you out next weekend, Theo." I turned and winked at Theo, the bartender who innocently flirted with me on a regular basis. It was all in fun, because I knew, like everyone else, that Theo's woman, Mabel, would mollywhop any woman who seriously tried to hit on her man. She could smell a man-stealing woman and would come out of the club's kitchen looking as mean as a snake. I stayed on Mabel's good side, because I am not really a fighter. I am also not a punk. I simply prefer to use my brain instead of my fists and fingernails.

"Catch you later, NikkiMac." Theo flashed his crooked smile my way as he continued rinsing bar glasses.

The loud music from Club Taste crashed into the quiet night as I clumsily pushed open the club's door. I mumbled to myself, "Maybe this cold air will sober me up some so I can safely drive home. No more partying for me tonight. Two drinks is my limit, but tonight I sucked up four gin and tonics. Got to drive home real slowly." I heard my heels clacking on the parking lot's asphalt. I saw my red Chevy about ten feet away; a black SUV was now parked very close to it. Then I saw the SUV's driver side door open and a man get out. He stepped into my path and blocked me from my car door.

"NikkiMac, you sure look good tonight. Good enough to take a little ride with me," Darius Muse said with a deep, slow drawl. He licked his bottom lip from corner to corner while staring at me suggestively. Darius Muse always sat at the dark end of the Club Taste bar. I never accepted the drinks he sent me because Darius made me nervous, always staring and licking his bottom lip.

"Excuse me, Mr. Muse, would you please move so I can open my car door? It's late and I have to get home." I spoke firmly and tried to cover my unease with a professional tone and a fake smile.

"So you do know my name, even though you've never accepted the friendly drinks I've sent to you. You have to get home for what? For who? I know you aren't married and you must not have a man, because you're here every weekend. NikkiMac, I'm not used to being ignored by the ladies." Darius leaned his body into mine and pushed me back against my car's driver side door. At first, I froze. My mind tried to register that this man had the nerve to actually touch me. I felt his arms reach around and hug me close against his slim, firm body. I felt his hard chest and muscular thighs; the arousal in his groin area. He seemed to enjoy the intimidation. He pressed his full lips against mine. I turned my head to the side to break kiss contact. So he slapped me across my cheek. It burned and my eyes watered. It felt like his handprint was etched into my cheek. Suddenly, rage roared up from my gut, surged into my chest, up in my throat, and into my mouth.

"Fool! You hit me! Who do you think you are?" I screamed, bared my teeth, and bit into the side of Darius' neck. I didn't see any, but I thought I tasted blood. Darius howled and pulled back his fist to punch me. Then I saw a flashlight's beam near the trunk of my car. A stocky older man with broad shoulders appeared behind Darius. "Where did he come from?" I thought.

"Young man, you need to leave this little lady alone. Back up, step aside, and let her get into her car so she can go." I said a silent prayer and scampered away from Darius. The older man, who I now saw had a silver gun with the barrel pointed downwards, gestured for me to come over to him. I quickly moved next to my rescuer.

"I'm sorry, Mr. Pace, no disrespect intended. She one of your people?" Darius rubbed his neck and walked to his car. He moved cautiously and respectfully while eyeing Mr. Pace's gun-toting right hand.

Mr. Pace addressed me. "What's your name, young lady?"

"I'm NikkiMac." I was glad to see this muscular, resolved, and armed senior citizen. To me, he looked like a chocolate, gray haired Superman. Mr. Pace focused on Darius.

"Man, you know better than to force yourself on a woman; you see she don't want you! Go on about your business, and don't let me catch you putting your hands on a woman again." Mr. Pace chuckled, "She bit the mess out of you, didn't she? It serves you right."

Darius drove off, but not without giving me a dirty look. "You might want to go to your doctor and get tested if you broke his skin and drew blood. Can't be too careful about body fluids these days. He ought to be glad you didn't call the police and press charges," fussed Mr. Pace.

"Oh no, I don't want to go through all that. My face will be alright. It wouldn't look good that I was out this late, leaving a bar, tipsy. I think my employer would frown on it."

"You're more worried about what your employer thinks than what you think of yourself?" He smiled gently, his gray mustache spread across his full top lip. "Sorry, young lady. I didn't mean to lecture; I know you're grown. My name is Foster Pace; I'm a Christian and a custodian at a church near here. I walk at night, that's the way I take my exercise, and also when I do some of my best thinking. Anyway, it's a good thing I cut through the plaza parking lot tonight, or Darius might have given you a lot more trouble. Got to be more careful, Miss NikkiMac. Are you all right to drive home?"

I shook my head from side to side, and started sniffling. It all came down on me then. "I'm so ashamed of myself. I know better than this. He could have raped me, killed me..." Mr. Pace put his arm around my shoulders.

"Stop crying. I'm going to take you home. You can get your car tomorrow when it's daytime and your head is clear. Miss NikkiMac, I'm just going to say this: God loves you. He wants what's good for you; this drinking and partying at clubs isn't good for you." Mr. Pace reached into his shirt pocket and pulled out a cloth handkerchief. "Here, take this and wipe your face." His voice was gentle; he was like a caring father talking to his young child. Next, he handed me a tract that briefly told about the church. Then he drove me to my home, watched me go inside, and drove off.

A few weeks later, I stepped inside the lobby of the church and walked right up to Mr. Foster Pace. He smiled broadly. "You finally made it, Miss NikkiMac. You'll be blessed for coming. Thank you for being here."

I observed the service and noted five distinct parts: congregational a cappella singing, prayer, communion, preaching, and offering. Minister Johnson met with me after service and explained about being baptized into Christ for the forgiveness of my sins. That really appealed to me, because I knew I'd sinned in my life. Most of my past sins I'd pretty much forgotten. But there were a couple I'd never been able to squash away; they nested in the secret parts of my soul...

In the twenty-fifth year of my life, I had a married lover. This man was older and supposedly wiser. We met at an Educators' Showcase Conference in his hometown of Philadelphia. For six months, he treated me to marvelous dinners, shows, and wonderful gifts. Greg said he was instantly attracted to my combination of intelligence and energy. I was instantly attracted to his lavish attention.

In less than a year, the bottom fell out.

"NikkiMac, you can't abort our baby! You can't take its life. This is so wrong!"

"No, Greg, what's wrong is me screwing around with a married man! I blame nobody but myself for that. I'm pregnant because of the one time I let you convince me a condom wasn't necessary. Well, once was all it took!" My body shook with anger. I sensed the tiny organism in my uterus pulling at me like a tight, possessive scab.

"NikkiMac, you know my wife is unable to have children. You can't kill the only child I might ever have!" Greg had the nerve to look pitiful. I wondered what I'd been thinking by hooking up with him.

"Have you lost your cotton-picking mind, Greg? I am at the beginning of my teaching career; I'm not about to raise a baby alone! You certainly can't do anything to help me; your wife would kill you! What am I supposed to do when I start showing and folks want to know about the baby's father? What about the child's questions about his or her father?"

His lips kept moving but I heard nothing that made any sense. I walked a few steps away from him, turned back, and announced, "Greg, tonight is the last time I intend for us to see or hear from each other. It was fun while it was fun, but now it's messy. I simply do not plan to have your baby." My hard expression told him that I was done with it and there was no need for him to say or do anything else.

The next day I went to the clinic and handled my business. The evidence of my sin was removed from my body, but not from my soul.

Would God forgive this?

When I was eight, I used to let a neighbor touch my budding breasts in exchange for money. His name was Mr. Manny, and this game was his idea. He was thirty-five, single, and almost cute. Our meetings happened the same way for almost a full summer. Once a week, he flew a certain flag on his flagpole over his front door. This was our signal. When I spotted that flag, I crept down the alley and entered his house through the unlocked back door. I walked over to the kitchen sink and stood facing him with my back to the sink. He rolled a low, creaky stool with one bad wheel over to me and sat on it in front of me. My part was to keep my hands at my sides and make no sounds while he did his thing.

"Let me touch your sweet puppies so they can grow," he whispered. Mr. Manny rubbed my breasts. He breathed heavily. He moaned. I smelled his medicated hair pomade and silently counted to one thousand. When it was over, he smiled. Then he handed me a folded twenty dollar bill.

"Go in peace, sweet girl. Remember, don't tell anyone!"

I never did tell. I knew it was wrong. I had been taught better, but I really wanted that money.

Our game ended when my mother sensed something, just the way perceptive mothers always do. I told her some kind of lie to cover myself and Mr. Manny. I didn't tell her about him touching my breasts for money, but she still commanded me to stay far away from Mr. Manny, and I did.

Years later, he was arrested and convicted for the rape and murder of a neighborhood girl. She was only five years old. Perhaps if I had told the truth, Mr. Manny would have been caught and locked up years before, and that little girl would have lived.

Would the God forgive me for these dark, secret sins?

I decided to give God a chance. On the following Sunday, I walked forward during the invitation song and repeated after Minister Johnson, "I believe that Jesus Christ is the Son of God." After changing into baptismal clothes in a dressing room, I walked down into the warm baptistery water. A brother waited for me there. He put one hand on my shoulder, raised his other hand and spoke out loud.

"Nikolis McQuaige, I baptize you in the name of the Father, the Son, and the Holy Spirit." He then whispered, "Hold your breath," leaned me back and underneath the water, and then lifted me back to a standing position. I was added to the church that day.

Today at age forty, I am still an active Christian, a member of the church. It's not a denomination; it's the church that one can read about in Acts chapter 2 of the Bible. It was established by Jesus Christ more than 2,000 years ago. There are no praise dancers, musical instruments, shouting, or getting "happy." We have communion every Sunday to commemorate Jesus Christ and His atoning sacrifice for mankind. We believe in full immersion baptism as the way into the body of Christ. One doesn't "join"; one is added to the church through baptism. At baptism, believers receive the gift of the Holy Spirit, who helps us do God's will. When Christ returns for His own, the faithful believers will live joyously and eternally in Heaven with the Godhead and the heavenly host. Those who don't belong to Christ will suffer eternal fiery punishment. The Bible is our guide in worship and in life. We believe it is the inspired word of God. We support the church by our monetary offerings. There are no earthly headquarters, because the church was established by Jesus and He is the head of the church.

My faith is important to me, but I'm not a holy roller. I attend Sunday church services and Wednesday night Bible study classes, but I don't reply, "I'm blessed!" whenever somebody asks, "How are you doing today, NikkiMac?" The way I understand the Bible, everyone is blessed by God in one way or another. Brother Pace often says, "If the good Lord allows you to see another day and you've got the ability to think, move your limbs, and breathe His air, you are blessed."

Chapter 3   Walking the Walk

Even though I struggle with some of my behaviors, and I've had my moments, I am encouraged by the fact that I'm still growing spiritually.

Jacee became a Christian about a year after I did. I think she noticed some positive changes in me. We sit on the same pew during worship services. We usually try hard to stay focused on the worship, but we sometimes become distracted. Every now and then during worship service or study classes, I allow myself to lose focus and let Satan appeal to my fleshly nature. It's not right, but it's true. This I do confess.

Whenever the saints come together to study or worship God, Satan also comes. He doesn't come to study the Bible or worship. He comes to cause problems and to disrupt the worship process. I guess he figures he has a room full of host bodies and minds, so what better place to be?

Sometimes he chooses people with the most potential for chaos, like Sister Batts. "Excuse me, Brother Teacher, but my research shows that you are wrong about this point. I am a Bible scholar, and I feel compelled to correct you publicly so that no babes in Christ will be led astray!" Sister Batts' deep, throaty voice rings out like this at least once a month during Bible study classes.

"Oh, not her dumb mouth again! I am so sick of her trying to teach the teacher!" The thought escapes my mouth in a soft whisper before I know it. I follow my words with a silent prayer for forgiveness; I struggle with my tongue. The Bible says the tongue is a little, but powerful, member of the human body and I am an example of that fact.

Satan also creeps up on folks who think they are the most pious. Anything Satan can do to take away focus from God and Jesus, Satan does. He enjoys the fact that some people are simply in the habit of going to church before doing anything else for which they've reserved their Sunday time. They sit and appear to daydream throughout the service. There are members who seem to tolerate the service so they can socialize with their church friends. They pass notes, share candy and gum. They pass babies back and forth. "Jumping up the babies," is what Brother Elton calls it. However, a lot of us are probably here because we are hurting from the cares of this world, and there's no place else to go for true relief. Church is a place where we feel we can get closer to God. All churches have their characters: people whose behavior makes you shake your head and wonder. My thought is that you should be on your best behavior when you come to worship, but maybe I'm being hypercritical. You can fool people, but God sees and knows everything about every one of us, all the time.

I enjoy being part of the worship experience each Sunday and the Bible study each Wednesday evening. It's never dull. Well, sometimes the preacher is long-winded. The church Announcements segment puts me into a temporary coma, but I revive. One of the old-time preachers says, "The church is a hospital for sinners. We all need Jesus." Statements like that from faithful seasoned members of the church help me, because I am sometimes harder on myself than God is. I observe personal improvement as I grow in Christ, but my fleshly nature often struggles with my spiritual nature, just as the Bible says in Galatians chapter 5, verse 17. When I scrutinize my compliance to God's word, my quick tongue, occasional lack of focus during worship, sometimes critical attitude, and not always under control sexual desire come to mind. I realize the need to yield to the Holy Spirit instead of trying to live a Christian life under my own power. I just mess up sometimes. Then, I ask for forgiveness and press on. On a positive note, my old party lifestyle is past, and cursing is no longer appealing for me to do or hear. Except for Jacee, I mostly hang out with a different social group since my baptism. I try to look nice, but not sexy. I realize that my worth is not measured by the number of men who desire me.

I squirm when I think of *The Walk of Shame* I took from Alexander Carson's apartment door to my car about at five in the morning some weeks ago. He's the one man from my party days that I touch base with sporadically. Alex has been my good male buddy for years. He makes me laugh like no other man does. He's more cute than he is fine. His skin is the color of cocoa and his build is wiry. Tall Alex has long arms, long fingers, great white teeth, and eyelashes so curly they make females jealous. Over the years, we have spent countless afternoons hanging out, going to the movies, dining, and just having fun. But one day, *just friends* became *friends with benefits*.

It wasn't planned. We were sitting on his sofa watching a romantic video. The characters caressed and then kissed. For some reason, we looked at each other and then did the same. Things progressed from there. After the deed was done, we were satisfied, but bewildered. That was the first of an odd pattern for Alex and me. We are not physical every time we meet, we mostly still pal around. However, after about six months of phoning and hanging out when we catch up with each other, we end up in bed together, and not sleeping. There are no strings attached; we call each other from time to time to check on each other's well being. I am not currently dating anyone, although I think Alex dates, and that's okay with me. But the subsequent guilt is not okay with me. Alex doesn't understand when I emote about it. We go back and forth with our positions.

"NikkiMac, don't feel so bad. We're just two good friends who sometimes give pleasure and comfort to one another. What can be so bad about that? We certainly respect each other, and we don't make love every time we get together, so we're not buck wild about this."

"Alex, you aren't a Christian, so you don't understand. I think you're a good person, I always have, but things in my life changed when I was added to the church. Behaviors that didn't bother me before do bother me now." After these exchanges, we agree to put some time and space between us until we embrace control in this area. We may speak on the phone, but not see each other for many months.

This is a struggle for me. I can't have a Christian influence on Alex if I'm intimate with him. That makes me a hypocrite and disobedient to God. I certainly can't fornicate with him and then try to evangelize him. I pray about this, and avoiding Alex seems to be the best strategy in light of our most recent episode. Meanwhile, I believe I'll get stronger and become so convicted of the sin of fornication that I'll choose to obey God rather than my libido.

Sometimes I consider handling this with church counseling, but my need for privacy stops me. I just can't see myself sitting in Minister Johnson's office telling him about me and Alex in bed doing the horizontal dance. Although, from the anonymous examples Brother Johnson cites in his teaching classes, he's heard it all. Lately, he's been teaching about Christian living, infusing his lessons with examples from his counseling sessions.

"Christian, if you are abusing your spouse, you are submitting to the flesh, not the Holy Spirit. I don't care if you use abusive words or commit physical abuse; it's carnal behavior that is not of the Spirit. Why do I have more than one couple meeting with me who report this abomination in their home? I'll tell you why; someone is living beneath their privilege in Christ Jesus. Someone is grieving the Holy Spirit. Men, the Bible tells us to love our wives like we love ourselves. Couples, the Bible tells us to submit to one another; to put each other's needs above our own. Living this way will prevent us from abusing each other. Let me put this in the pot and stir it: if you think you can abuse your spouse and get away with it because the church doesn't know what happens in your home, you've got another think coming! The church may not know. You may be fronting when you get here. But God knows; He's omniscient. He knows everything." Brother Johnson surely cannot be accused of failing to tell us what the Bible says. He respects the privacy of his counselees, but he puts the behavior out there in order to take us out of the clouds. He is a proponent of practical Christian living.

"Another situation that requires a lot of my counseling time is grown Christian folks who are shacking up! If you live with someone in a romantic way that you are not legally married to, you are disobeying the word of God. Sisters, I don't understand how you can let some no-account man who doesn't love you enough to marry you be all up in your bed and snore in your face every night. Brothers, ask yourselves if you'd like for your daughter to be shacking up with a man who refuses to marry her. If you wouldn't like that, then you shouldn't be living that way with someone else's daughter. God tells us in scripture about the honor that is found in marriage and about the judgment coming to those who ignore His command. Write down Hebrews chapter 13, verse 4. If you don't have anything to write with, get the tape or CD and listen to it when you get home. I'm not making this up. It's the will of God." Brother Johnson may be stepping on some toes, but I believe he does so with love.

"Here's another issue that comes into my office: one Christian not being able to get along with another Christian. Sometimes it's gossip that causes a problem between two people. Sometimes it's just plain envy.

This should not be heard of in the Lord's house. The Bible gives us clear guidance on how to resolve conflicts. It also makes it clear that we are to love one another. You can't love God if you hate your fellow Christian. First John chapter 4, verses 20 through 21 make it plain. And while I'm here, let me go further. You also can't love God if you hate someone who's not a Christian. You may, and rightfully so, hate sinful behavior."

I've got a way to go, but at least I can look back and see I've left some sinful behaviors behind.

Chapter 4   Too Much Information

Jacee and I get out of her car five minutes before 11:00 am service, so we walk quickly. We want to be seated before service starts. Wouldn't you know it? Cletus, a neighborhood alcoholic, darts from across the street and meets us on the church steps. He moves so fast that he makes his own wind.

"Hey, NikkiMac! Girl, you still look good! You never get old! Look at that pretty skin. Listen, can you let me hold a dollar? I ain't had nothin' to eat since yesterday!" His breath is kicking and giving me a one, two, punch, so I back up before I respond.

"Cletus, I thought you were still in rehab. I don't have any change. Anyway, when are you going to come inside this building to hear the gospel instead of hustling church folk outside?"

"Aw, NikkiMac, I'm gonna come to church when I get a suit. I don't wanna come lookin' all raggedy. You got any change? Come on, please?" His runny eyes belie the energy of his begging. His clothes don't match and his dark brown skin has a shiny purple tint. Cletus is about my age; I know we both attended Trenton Central High School. I think he was one or two grades ahead of me. He was a talented and popular star on the track team. That's some of what I know about him. What I don't know much about is the path that led him from track star to where he is today. Cletus has been to rehab and jail so many times that it makes me wonder about the success of either institution.

"Let's go, NikkiMac, we're going to be late." Jacee lightly tugs my arm. She has no sympathy for Cletus. I toss him a dollar and a warning.

"Cletus, the Lord will know if you use this money for something to drink, and not for food."

"I swear I'm gonna get food, NikkiMac." Cletus does a little dance and darts away as fast as he showed up.

17

Jacee and I make it through the auditorium doors just in time. Another second and the two ushers would have made us wait in the lobby until after opening prayer. One of them rolls his eyes at us as we whiz by. He takes his job very seriously.

"Good morning, brothers, sisters, and visitors. We are about to begin our morning worship service. Before the reading of scripture, are there any prayer requests?" From the pulpit, Brother Flowers pauses and looks over the congregation. Three people stand up.

Sister Pearl speaks, "I'd like to ask prayer for one of the ladies on my job. She's scheduled for heart surgery tomorrow and she just lost her husband to cancer three months ago." Sympathetic noises follow Sister Pearl's request.

Next, Brother Elton speaks. I have an idea of what his request is about, because he makes the same one almost every Sunday. "Please pray for me on my job, because my supervisor got the *devil* in her! She keeps hollerin' at me and tellin' me that I stink." I suppress a giggle, not because I think it's cool that Brother Elton's supervisor is mean to him, but the way he says it is funny. I know for a fact that he doesn't stink, but he sometimes looks like he does.

What he's regularly guilty of is blowing out the restroom near the Nursery every Sunday morning. The uninitiated folks walk into a fume cloud, gag, and exclaim, "Whew, what died in here?" The initiated wisely use the other restrooms. I found this out the hard way.

Brother Cliff is next. "Brothers and sisters, I have sinned. I have repented of my sin, and I ask the prayers of the church." He turns around and points directly at Sister Hobson. "I have committed the sin of fornication with Sister Hobson." I hear gasps and unsympathetic noises. Sister Hobson looks stunned, gets up, and walks quickly out of the auditorium. Our minister's wife, Sister Sharlette Johnson, rushes out to assist Sister Hobson. My right hand clasps my bowed forehead as I lean forward and slowly nod my head from side to side. It's 11:10 in the morning and I have already assumed *The Position*.

Jacee leans over to me, "I don't believe Brother Cliff put Sister Hobson on blast like that! The confession should be as public as the sin. They fornicated, but I was not there and do not need to have that picture in my head. Why didn't they just ask each other and God for forgiveness and stop having sex with each other or anyone else until they're married?"

"Shh," I interrupt Jacee, who can go on forever. One problem is she doesn't really know how to whisper, so people all around can hear what she's saying. The other problem is I have empathy for the fornicators. I've been there and done that, and sometimes I still do it. I'm not proud of it, though.

I know this one thing for sure: Sister Sharlette is exactly the person that Sister Hobson needs right now. Our minister's wife has a comforting, nonjudgmental presence. She helped me a few years ago when I was feeling sad about my parents' absence. It was a church Family Day, and I felt like the only orphan present. My eyes were moist as we sang; I didn't interact much with others. I couldn't control my pre-bawling shoulder shakes. Worse yet, I was ashamed of my grown behind for feeling this way. Sister Johnson noticed my demeanor. She approached and guided me to an unoccupied classroom. She listened intently while I unburdened myself about missing Alice and Nickson McQuaige.

"Sister NikkiMac, you'll always carry them with you, because they are alive in your memory and in your heart. It doesn't matter how old we are, we never lose the yearning for our departed loved ones. Every now and then, give yourself time to embrace that fact. Then pray, thanking God for sharing them with you. Ask Him for strength to carry on. God loves you, and God will comfort you." I leaned my head on her ample bosom; it was like being on a 44DD pillow made with that special spring back foam. She kept hugging me until I was alright, and she never again mentioned my small meltdown. Now, she simply smiles warmly at me whenever she sees me being quiet and raises one eyebrow as if to say, "You okay, NikkiMac?" I always wink a "Yes, my dear sister" signal back to her. I am glad Sister Sharlette is my big sister in Christ.

The sound of whispering moves across the auditorium, but not for long, because Brother Flowers clears his throat and gets the attention of the congregation. "Let's bow our heads in reverence to God. We need to go to Him in prayer."

Chapter 5   Give Me Strength

Jacee is on a roll. "Look at that visitor with those two little kids, marching down to the front of the church for a seat! Why do people with their noisy babies always sit on the front pews? The babies fret and holler right in Brother Johnson's face while he's preaching. Every time the preacher raises his voice, the babies raise theirs." Her fake whispering draws attention from people sitting nearby.

"Stop it, Jacee," I whisper back. "Pick up your songbook and sing." She rolls her eyes at me and snatches a hymnal from the holder in front of us. I wonder why she's so cranky this morning, until I get distracted. Brother Leethan, the song leader for today, is repeating the first verse of *Where He Leads I'll Follow*. The congregation complies, until Brother Vonner takes over from his seat and bellows out verses two and three. We now follow Brother Vonner, who has taken the song away from Brother Leethan. I finally figure out that Brother Leethan has memorized the words to verse one only. I suspect that the brother needs eyeglasses to clearly read the words from the songbook. It seems like he's memorized all the words to about ten songs. If an extra song is needed, Brother Leethan repeats a verse or fronts. He calls a hymn number, smiles at the congregation and says, "You start it off, and I'll catch up." His voice is quite good. We support him because he's so humble, and he loves to lead songs.

Minister Johnson's sermon today is about Job, the man the Bible describes as blameless, upright, and reverent before God. "So one day, Christian friends and visitors, the angels came before God, and guess who came with them? Satan came! God asked Satan where he'd been. Satan replied that he'd been roaming around, going back and forth in the earth. Now, him being Satan, we all know that he wasn't roaming around doing anything positive. No! Satan was looking for somebody to accuse before God, and God offered Job as a faithful servant. Satan did not like the fact that God delighted in Job's devotion. He wanted to break the bond between God and Job. Satan told God that Job was only righteous because God had abundantly blessed Job. Satan told God to stop blessing Job, and then watch Job curse God. But God vouched for Job and faced Satan's accusation against His servant. God and Satan had a conversation. Consider this, my brothers and sisters: what conversations might God have with Satan about you?"

I get a lump in my throat when I hear this. In my current lifestyle, would God defend me before Satan? I'm fairly righteous, but I know I could and should be better. I've been in the church for about ten years now. I don't visit the sick often, and I surely don't visit in the prisons. In James chapter 1, the Bible lists attributes of pure religion that I still aspire to reach. I give ten percent of my gross salary in the church offering and I am working on increasing that amount. I need to work on my attitude with people who annoy me. I'm swift with verbal retaliation, and that's not good. I also fornicate sometimes. These thoughts make me uncomfortable; the discomfort activates my bladder. I whisper to Jacee, "Excuse me; I need to go the restroom," before I move past her to exit the pew. Usher Gray scowls at me as I scoot past him. He never wants anyone out of their seat. I travel across the lobby and down the hallway to the ladies restroom.

Inside the restroom, I smell her before I see her, and the smell is not good. Mad Maggie, a neighborhood homeless woman, is at one of the sinks. She's giving herself a birdbath. Every now and then, she comes into the building and goes to the restroom to wash her body. She stays there until someone escorts her out. Today, her funk is so fierce that my eyes begin to water. This is the odor of old, rank urine, mixed with stale sweat and sour clothing. Mad Maggie's head is wrapped in two or three scarves and she's wearing at least two sweaters with the sleeves pushed up to her boney elbows. The skin on her face is caramel in color, with a shiny reddish tint that probably comes from all the liquor she drinks. Her droopy bottom lip is dark around the rim, but it's bright pink in the fleshy part. It looks like every other tooth in her mouth is either rotten or missing. I'm not sure about the foot gear, which looks like sneakers inside plastic bags with rubber bands wrapped around the ankles. Tall and thin, Mad Maggie is mostly clothes and a bad attitude. I try not to stare or get too close. People say she will curse you out and even hit out at you if you get her rattled.

"Hello, how are you today, M'am?" I try to sound as if she belongs here doing what she's doing.

"I'm minding my own business, if you must know!" she huffs at me.

I think, "Your nasty butt has no business here in the first place, washing your face and your other body parts with our church paper towels." But I keep my peace, enter the stall farthest away from her, and leave Mad Maggie alone. Holding my breath as much as I can, I take care of my business, wash my hands, and leave.

Outside, I bump into Brother Carlos as he leaves the men's restroom. He's a friendly thirty-something brother with a wicked sense of humor. He walks close to me and whispers, "Don't shake Brother Elton's hand. I'm not kidding, don't shake his hand." I smile and get ready to ask why at the same time Brother Elton exits the men's restroom.

"How are you, Sister NikkiMac?" Brother Elton smiles and offers me his right hand. I cut my eyes quickly at Brother Carlos.

"Good afternoon, dear brother. Good to see you today." I give Brother Elton a quick butterfly hug, the kind where you lean in and out really fast. My arms stay at my sides. That gesture works; the brother smiles broadly and moves on.

"You'd better be glad you didn't shake his hand, NikkiMac. I was in the restroom while he was in there. He did Number Two and he didn't even wash his hands when he finished. I knew he was going to shake hands with people. That's just stank. He's got the Dookey Hand, and I saved you from the Dookey Touch." Brother Carlos turns and walks off, laughing at his own joke.

When I get to the door of the auditorium, I tap Usher Gray on the arm and tattle, "There's a homeless woman funking up the ladies restroom. Why don't you check on that?" Then, I walk promptly to my seat next to Jacee and sit down. Brother Martin is about to begin the announcements. Today, I try harder to pay attention.

"There will be a meeting of the Helpful Hands Committee immediately after worship today in Classroom 1." I notice two people pack up their Bibles, coats, and leave their seats. I guess they figure that since the sermon is over, church is over, and there's no need to hear the announcements.

"There will be a Youth Committee meeting today after worship in Classroom 2." Jacee yawns. I tap her on the knee before she begins to stretch.

"Please sign up on the sheet in the lobby for the church picnic trip to Family Fun Place. The cost is thirty-five dollars. See any member of the Friendship Committee if you have any questions. Let me just say something about this. Please don't pay for the trip ticket before you give your weekly offering to the Lord. Let us keep our priorities straight." Brother Martin pauses and looks over the congregation, showing his amused fatherly smile.

"Sister Mamie Lou's black fur jacket is missing. She says she put it on the coat rack in the lobby last Sunday morning, and it was not there after service. Please return our sister's black fur jacket right away. Check your closets at home; maybe someone grabbed the wrong coat by mistake. Although, I will say that you should know whether or not a coat is yours by the coat's look, smell, or fit. If you know you don't own a black fur coat, and now there's one in your closet, you need to bring it back. If you don't bring it back, that's called stealing, and the Bible tells us that stealing is a sin. I know you didn't ask for all that, but it didn't cost you a thing." Jacee and I chuckle; we know from experience at this congregation that our senior Brother Martin is a straight shooter.

"I have a few more announcements, so please bear with me. Please don't park in the marked Handicapped spaces out front unless you are truly handicapped. I know you may be running late and those spaces are close to the door, but they are by law designated for handicapped people coming to our building. Violators, take heed. The Lord may make you so you really need to use those handicapped spaces, you know what I mean? That's all I'm going to say on that."

People are starting to get restless; there are a few more escapees. Janey, the six-year-old in front of me, stands up and turns to face her mother. She puts on her little coat, hat, and attitude. "Mommy, can we go home now? I'm ready to eat."

Janey's mom tries to shush her, "Church is almost over, Janey. Here, eat this mint. We'll be leaving soon."

Janie takes the mint from her mom and pops it into her mouth. Her expression says, "Okay for now, Mommy, but when this mint is gone, we'll both be leaving." I smile at the little girl; she's got a cute, round face. Her big brown eyes dwarf a little pug nose and bow-like lips. She responds to my smile with a slow small wave. I enjoy children. Adults, often not so much.

Brother Martin's waving hand brings me back into focus. "Someone lost these car keys. I will give them to Brother Pace; you can see him after we dismiss." People start checking their pockets and purses.

"Also, there's a real nice lost pen up here. I want to make sure it is returned to its rightful owner. If you give me an accurate description of it, I'll know it's yours, and then you can have it back."

Chapter 6   Cletus' New Clothes

"NikkiMac, I love you, my sister, but you do not know how to park a car."

"Oh, just you shut up, Jacee." I back my car into the parking space in the church's lot, and look in my driver's side rear mirror. I check the white lines painted on the asphalt so I can park straight and in between them. I hate to back out of any parking space; pulling out is more my thing. I finally get it right, and we exit. Jacee walks ahead while I check to see if both car doors are locked. I purchased this car with driver side remote features only, because I figured I'd be mostly riding alone. Plus, it was less expensive that way. Jacee thinks I'm cheap. I think I'm frugal. Out of the corner of my eye I see the boney legs of Cletus quickly carrying him in my direction. I decide to ignore him.

"NikkiMac, hold up, I got something to tell you!" Jacee turns back, looks disgusted and goes inside the building. My feet keep moving toward the door, but fast-moving Cletus catches up to me.

"Cletus, I don't want to be late for worship service. What is it?"

"NikkiMac, I got a church suit from Mr. Foster Pace!"

I am glad for Cletus, but not thrilled with his boozy breath, which threatens to singe my eyebrows and other facial hair. I pull my head back, but Cletus doesn't seem to notice. He continues speaking, more rapidly than usual. "While I was walking past the building last night, I saw Mr. Pace's truck parked outside. I felt like talking, and he always speaks to me when he sees me. He seems like someone who cares, something like you, NikkiMac. I know I get on your nerves, but at least you usually speak to me and invite me to church like I have the right to be inside a church. I know I'm not living right. But I don't hurt nobody but me. I stay in a room at my mom's house not far from here. She's eighty years old, and I try to help her out. She don't approve of my drinking and she don't feed me. Mom just gives me a place to lay my head, and that's fine with me, because I hate sleeping in homeless shelters."

I've heard some disturbing things about people in shelters having to sleep with one eye open, so others don't steal their belongings. Although most of the stuff I see the local homeless people carting around in wagons and shopping carts looks like junk to me, it seems to be treasure to them.

"Anyway, I had the feeling that Mr. Pace would be a cool dude to have a conversation with. So I knocked on the church door, he opened it and I stepped inside. I walked around with him as he cleaned the building, and I was talking my fool head off. You know what, NikkiMac? Mr. Pace listened to me last night like I was somebody worth listening to. He didn't judge me. He asked a few questions that let me know he was listening. He asked me when I was coming back inside the church for worship, and I told him I didn't have a suit to wear. So he took me to the Clothing Bank in the church's annex, helped me pick out a sharp navy blue suit, a white shirt, and a pinstriped tie. Then he then gave me socks, shoes, even underwear!"

Emotion causes Cletus' ashy face to soften, his eyes tear, his nose runs. My heart goes out to him; I can't brusquely break this conversation so I can get inside on time. God loves us all, and that includes Cletus, who has more to say.

"But NikkiMac, I am ashamed of this one thing. Last night, Mr. Pace gave me the invitation and the clothes I need for church, and I should have gone home with my free clothes so I could sleep and be ready for church. I didn't do that, though. I took my clothes to my room in Mom's house and then I went back out in the streets. I wound up in the alley with some guys who had lots of booze. It was there; it was free, and we sucked it down until we all passed out. I woke up in the alley and rushed here to tell you. I'm so sorry I messed up. Please tell Mr. Pace what happened, because I feel ashamed to look at him right now. Tell him I'll be inside the church, bright-eyed and bushy-tailed next Sunday morning. I'm for real, NikkiMac."

Speechless, I watch Cletus spin around and bump into Sister Melody, who is walking to the building. "Oh Miss, I'm so sorry. I would never bump into such a lovely lady as you on purpose." He may be an alcoholic, but he still can turn on the charm.

Sister Melody fixes her frown when she hears the compliment about her beauty. "That's okay," she says, as she smiles, waves at me, and moves inside the church doors. Sister Melody is our congregation's walker, our stroller. During services, she routinely gets up and strolls up and down the center aisle. Sister Melody goes out for a drink of water from the lobby fountain, and back to her seat. Sister Melody goes out to hang up her sweater. She walks serenely; it's a slow Miss America walk. A small smile moves across her face as she travels. The ushers roll their eyes at her in irritation, because she continuously violates their Sit Down rule. She doesn't seem to notice. Sister Melody often goes out to the restroom.

We had an encounter there one time. I'd reluctantly gone there during service because I could no longer hold my water. Sister Melody was all up in the mirror as I did the pee-pee dance into one of the stalls.

"Sister NikkiMac, how are you this fine Sunday morning?"

"I'm much better now that I'm passing this water, Sister Melody."

"Good. Now come on out here and tell me if this shade of lipstick looks good on me. Someone told me that deep red doesn't look right on women with dark complexions, but I bought it anyway. My boyfriend says it makes me look cheap, but I still like it. No matter how nice I think I look when I get to church, I must keep checking in this church mirror. I'm just too much, don't you think?"

Since I figured this was a soliloquy, and not a conversation, I said a couple of polite words to Sister Melody, did my bathroom business, and hurried back to the auditorium for worship.

Chapter 7   Tasha Pace, Prayer Requests, and Communion

Because it's my turn to set up the communion trays, I'm at the church building early this Sunday morning. I notice Brother Pace tidying up the front lawn, so I start to walk in his direction. Before I can reach him, his daughter Tasha zips around from the back of the building. She's walking her fast, jerky, arm-swinging crack head walk. She annoys the heck out of me. I wonder why such a good man has a skank like that for a daughter. She reaches him; it looks like she's asking for something. I pause, close enough to listen, but out of their field of vision.

Brother Pace responds to his daughter's request, "I'm sorry, Tasha, but you have to leave my house, I can't help you anymore. You are causing nothing but hurt with your lying, drug abuse, and your thieving ways. I am just glad your mother isn't alive to see how you turned out. Lord knows she and I did not raise you to be like this. We did the same for you as we did for your brother John and your sister Lukey. Look at their lives, and look at yours. They have been in the church since their early teen years; and they are faithful. John is in the army fighting for our country. Lukey is just twenty-five and has her own place in Philadelphia, a job, and a car. She's active in the church. Tasha, you're the oldest, you were added to the church when you were a teenager, and now you are the worse off. You left the Lord and won't let Him change your life."

Tasha shifts from one foot to the other as her father talks. "Daddy, you know I am trying to do better," she protests. She sounds whiny and insincere.

"Listen to me; I can't have you in my living space. Because you steal, I have to warn my visitors to watch their wallets and not sit their pocketbooks down in the house when you're around. You always want folks to let you have some of their hard-earned money or give you a ride somewhere. All you do is take; you never give anything but grief. When you enter a room, you suck all the air out of it. I have to protect myself and others from you. I don't know what else to do but continue to pray for you; I've done everything else. Yes, Tasha, you do have to leave my house tonight. Meet me here after evening service and I'll drive you to the house to get your few things. There is no need to give me your house key; I'm changing the locks tonight after you leave." I see the pain and resolve on his face and start moving toward him. Tasha jerks around when she hears my footsteps.

"Hey, long time, no see, Sister NikkiMac. How are you making out?" I move closer to the two of them as Brother Pace nods to acknowledge my presence. There's leathery skin on her thin face. Her lips are crookedly drawn on her face with bright red lipstick. Dry brown hair with blond streaks stands up on her head. I can't figure out her eyes; one of them looks surprised and the other one doesn't. Tasha's mouth moves animatedly, "So NikkiMac, let me hold a dollar. I know you got a dollar, as rich as you lookin' today."

My hands ball into fists, and I want to pop her in the mouth for coming here embarrassing Brother Pace. "Sorry, Tasha, the only money I have on me is for the church offering." I smile at Brother Pace; he nods sadly at me and briskly walks to the church's storage shed. He drags the broom behind him. Tasha blinks as she watches him walk away. Then, she looks at me with a crazy grin.

"See you later, NikkiMac. Maybe I can get a dollar from you next time." Her quick, jerky walk takes her away from the church grounds. She reminds me of a poorly drawn cartoon character.

I stop looking at his departing daughter and think about Brother Pace. I guess he's about sixty-five or seventy years old. He's been a widower for some years. He's the sweetest, wisest Christian man I know. He surely helped me take a second thought about my life. He's still a handsome man and I see a few of the older sisters here send signals out to him, but he doesn't appear to notice. It would be nice if he found righteous companionship again. It might help to balance the disappointment of having a trifling daughter like Tasha.

"Beep, beep!" The sound of Jacee's car horn brings me back. She's here to help me with the communion trays this morning. Inside the church's kitchen, we get busy putting small, clear plastic cups into the openings of shiny brass trays. Then we fill the cups with grape juice. Unleavened crackers are placed in the brass plates. The trays are covered and taken to the communion table in the auditorium. We don't have to, but Jacee and I do this in silence. After we complete our task, we head to the auditorium for worship.

Brother Carlos stands before the audience. "It is time for us to begin our worship service. Are there any requests for prayer? If so, please stand so I can acknowledge you. I'll start on my right, and then move to my left, so we can do this in an orderly way."

Jacee elbows me. "What's Carlos doing up there, with his silly self? Where's Brother Flowers?"

"Cut it out, Jacee. You know Carlos can be serious when he has to be." I am hoping that his crazy side won't surface while he's up there in the pulpit, but I won't admit this to Jacee.

Brother Elton, rarely one to miss an opportunity for prayer requests, speaks. "Please pray for me on my job, because my supervisor lied on me this week and reported me for being late to work. I want to hate her, but I know God does not want me to hate people, so pray for me. Thank you."

Brother Cliff stands up, and I hold my breath. The last time he asked for prayer, he confessed to fornication with Sister Hobson. That was a hot mess.

"I ask for prayer because I have been late to church for the past four Sundays. I don't know what it is; I just can't seem to get here on time."

Brother Carlos' crazy kicks in. "Well, brother, you made it here on time this morning to ask for prayer. What did you do differently this morning than you did the last four Sunday mornings?"

I bow my head and prepare to assume *The Position*. Jacee whispers, "Oh no he didn't!"

Brother Cliff looks confused. "I have to think about that, brother."

"I'll tell you what, how about I call you when I get up next Sunday morning? I volunteer to be your personal Sunday morning alarm clock until you get this under control." Brother Carlos smiles broadly at Brother Cliff. A few chuckles are heard as the stunned brother wordlessly takes his seat. I guess he'll think twice before making a frivolous prayer request next time.

"Is there anyone to my left with a request?" Brother Carlos signals to Sister Mamie Lou. She's a sister who came out of a church where they shout and jump about during services. She sometimes forgets that we don't do that here, so she occasionally waves her hands in the air, claps, and shakes her head so hard that her wig moves back and forth and from side to side. It looks like it's trying to keep up with her head. I often wonder why she doesn't pin her wig down. One time, she got so carried away with her rejoicing that she bent all the way forward and her wig just plain flopped off. When she stood up straight, the only thing her head was wearing was a stocking cap. It was a memorable moment.

"Thank you, brother. I want to give thanks to all of you for praying for me. I have been on the sick list for about two months now. I was not able to come out to church on the regular because I was too sick. The doctors at first didn't know what was wrong with me. One day I was fine, the next I was flat on my back. It turns out I became allergic to a medication I used to take and almost died! All I can say is if you do not believe in the power of God, you need to get your head examined; you belong in a mental hospital! I'm not fully recovered, but I am able to come to church. Please keep me in your prayers, because God is so good."

"All the time!"

"Amen!"

"I know that's right, Sister Mamie Lou. We are so thankful you are feeling better and are able to be with us again." No one else stands for prayer, so Brother Carlos asks us to bow our heads. He then leads us in a heartfelt prayer.

Brother Vincent, today's song leader, is upbeat. The congregation is always uplifted by his style of singing. He has near-perfect pitch, and doesn't drag the songs. Brother Vincent uses the right tempo, enthusiasm, and sincerity. After three hymns, a brother leads us in the reading of scripture. We sing three more hymns. At the end of *I Gave My Life for Thee*, five brothers enter the auditorium in single file. They are leading us in today's communion. Brother Martin begins, "We will now celebrate the death, burial, and resurrection of our Lord and Savior Jesus Christ. Let us remember what He has done for us. He died for the forgiveness of our sins. We take our example from Acts chapter 20, verses 5 through 7. We continue with First Corinthians chapter 11, verses 23 through

32." He reads the verses aloud while we read our Bibles silently. "Brother Dexter, please pray for the bread, which represents the body of Christ."

Brother Dexter bows his head and prays. "Our Father in heaven, your name is holy. Please bless this bread. I pray that those who partake of it will do so with clean hands and hearts. Amen." The congregation responds.

Brother Martin continues, "Brother Pace, please pray for the fruit of the vine, which represents the blood of Christ."

Brother Pace bows his head and prays. "Heavenly Father, thank you for the blood of Christ that was shed for the remission of our sins. I pray that those who receive it will do so in a manner that is pleasing to You. Amen." The congregation responds. The five brothers then take communion themselves, before moving the trays around the room in a set pattern. They make sure that all Christians receive communion. I have my breath mint ready, because the purple grape juice produces on the tongue what we call "communion breath." It's pretty tart.

It's interesting to me how babies and young children are fascinated by the communion trays and what's in them. As the trays are passed along the pews, babies reach for the crackers and juice like they are the best candy and soda around. Toddlers whine," Mommy, I want some juice!" and sometimes get popped when they put up a fuss. One sister has a good routine. When the communion trays reach her pew, she quickly gives her two-year-old a baggie that contains about four animal crackers and a tiny juice box. This distracts him from the communion trays, and he still feels like he's part of the action.

Chapter 8 Clara Lee Gets Baptized

"Christians, your motivation to serve God should be to return His love. It shouldn't only be that you're afraid to *not* obey Him." Minister Johnson's message makes me think, because sometimes the only reason I do what is right is to avoid God's punishment. I do not want to go to Hell, but that shouldn't be the only reason I serve God. I think about some of the things He's done for me. I've got life and I'm in the body of Christ. I'm healthy, have a decent job, and a solid sister friend in Jacee. I have a house, a working car, and a warm Christian family. I still miss my parents, but I haven't had them since I was in my twenties. First, my mom, Alice McQuaige, was defeated by breast cancer. It took her quickly after it was diagnosed. Mom had the biggest heart; she'd give you the shirt off her back if it would help you. Nickson McQuaige, my dad, developed ALS and struggled with that monster for five years. I remember the regular visits to the nursing home. Near the end, Dad could only blink to communicate to me, his only child. Those were hard times for me. Both of my parents called themselves Baptists and were good people, but neither attended church regularly. I'm thankful and know I was blessed to have their love, rearing, and support in my early and teen years. But in my twenties, I had no Mom, no Dad, and no spiritual base.

A chirping sound from above pulls me from my reverie. I hear chirps, a pause, and a series of tweets. The sound pattern continues as Brother Johnson preaches. People whisper and look up. Above us in the ceiling, some birds have built a nest between the drop ceiling and the roof. They are not visible, but they are definitely loud. I didn't notice them during congregational singing, but now they seem to accent Brother Johnson's message.

"In closing, fellow Christians, the Bible tells us that if we practice the presence of God in our daily walk, we will not fall into sin."

"Chirp! Tweet! Tweet! Tweet!"

"So the birds have come to worship, and even they agree with the Lord! They've been singing this morning. If you haven't been singing during our song service this morning, the birds put you to shame." Brother Johnson looks up and points in the direction of the sound. We all lift our heads and say, "Amen."

Brother Johnson closes out his sermon and we stand for the song of invitation, which today is *Lord, I'm Coming Home.* As we end the third verse, a lady visitor begins a tentative walk down the center aisle toward Brother Johnson's outstretched arms. "Praise the Lord! We have a soul who wants to be baptized into Christ this morning! Is there anybody else who wants to come on home to Him? Whosoever will, let them come." By the end of the song, the visitor stands facing our minister. Brother Johnson asks the woman her name.

"My name is Clara Lee," she replies loudly. She's the hefty woman I noticed earlier. Throughout the service, she vigorously rocked herself back and forth. At first, I thought it was because she felt cold, but now I see something about the set of her face and her outfit that strongly suggests, "I have special needs." She is wearing a pair of plaid pajama bottoms that are too short and tight in the butt area. Her shirt has black and white polka dots. Her oversized red jacket looks like it's made for a man. Furry bunny slippers are on her feet; the bunnies' heads are flopped over to the side like they've given up the battle for good posture. Her hair is plaited in at least fifty little sections, each one squared off with the short plait standing up in the middle. It reminds me of an aerial view of some farm crops.

"Clara Lee, if you believe these words, please repeat them after me: I believe that Jesus Christ is the Son of God." Brother Johnson pauses for Clara's response.

"I believe that Jesus Christ is the Son of God."

"Amen!" rings out from the congregation, almost like one grand, joyful voice.

"Clara Lee, this confession you made brought death to Christ, but will bring life to you after you have completed your obedience through baptism. At your baptism, you will be added by Christ into His body. You will receive the gift of the Holy Spirit who will guide you in living a faithful life on this earth. Continue on in the Lord, and heaven will one day be your eternal home. Let us prepare for the baptism. Clara, please follow Sister Johnson, who will help you dress for baptism."

Brother Johnson prompts, "Let the congregation say 'Amen', because a soul has decided to accept the Lord as her Savior!" We all do that with joy.

I take a mental trip back to my baptism years ago and recall the routine at this congregation. A designated brother or sister takes you to a small dressing room, where you remove your clothes, put on a white pair of thick cotton pants and a karate-style jacket. The fabric is heavy enough so that when you come up out of the water you are not showing all of your assets in wet, clingy cloth. That would not be too cool in a spiritual setting. Ladies are given a swim cap so their hairdos are protected from the water. At my baptism, for some crazy reason, I couldn't decide whether to take my panties off or leave them on before I entered the water. I made the wrong choice and spent my first hour as a Christian with no drawers on. Sister Sharlette discreetly put my wet panties on the radiator in the back so they could quickly dry during service. This act rescued my bare bottom before I left for home. The thought makes me chuckle, and I bring my mind back to the service.

While we sing another hymn, the ushers begin collecting the offering. Our baptism pool is behind the raised pulpit and is covered by vertical fabric blinds. While Clara is being assisted in the dressing room, Usher Gray assumes his important task of holding onto the curtain cord so he can open the curtains when Clara descends into the water and the waiting arms of Brother Sanders. He's been selected to do the baptizing this week. Following the collection of the offering, Brother Martin steps up to read the announcements, but the usher signals the baptism's beginning. As the usher opens the curtains, we see Clara standing next to Brother Sanders. It's quite obvious that she is a lot bigger and heavier than Brother Sanders.

Here goes Jacee. "Why is that little brother going to baptize this Clara? Why doesn't one of the bigger men do it? How is he going to lift her big butt up from underneath the water?"

"Shut up, Jacee. Water makes you lighter and God will make a way." I am thinking the same thing, though. This should be interesting.

When Brother Sanders gets to, "I now baptize you in the name of the Father, the Son, and the Holy Spirit," and leans Clara backwards under the water, she starts to freak. I guess she thinks she is going to drown. She gets immersed, but starts thrashing around as the brother tries to pull her back up.

"Aieyee!" Clara squeals.

Brother Sanders assures, "You're alright. Put your leg down!" That leg is surely sticking straight up in the air, momentarily keeping Brother Sanders from standing Clara back up. But the brother digs down deep into his strength reserves and manages to get Clara into a two-footed standing position. We almost applaud. I want to hold up a perfect 10 scorecard for his Herculean effort. Sister Clara Lee is now a member of the church.

Amen and Amen.

Chapter 9   Feeding the Hungry

On one Saturday of each month, our congregation feeds and provides clothing for the less fortunate in the community. First they eat, and then we invite them to our Clothing Bank, where they can choose free clean donated clothing and shoes. Their selections are bagged, and they are given containers of takeout food. Religious tracts are offered, but not forced on our guests. We also provide counseling and information about city agencies that can assist our guests. Brother Johnson often reminds us of Jesus' words in Matthew chapter 25, verses 34 through 46. These words inspire many of us to put effort into feeding and clothing the less fortunate.

The doors of our church annex open at 12 noon to a line of people of all ages and both sexes. Some come with their children. Some are around my age. Jacee and I often volunteer to assist, so today we are here with our aprons, gloves, and hairnets. We are putting paper plates filled with food on the numbered tables. Today's menu is spaghetti and meat balls, bread rolls, a small garden salad, and fresh fruit. Our guests also get to choose a dessert from a separate table.

"All right, we are about to open the door," Brother Pace says and smiles at the volunteers. There's a rush to get the bread baskets on the last one of the twenty tables. Brother Sampson opens the door and the people begin to come inside.

"Welcome, ladies and gents," says Brother Pace. "Please have seat and we'll have prayer before eating." The crowd shuffles in; they are mostly quiet and pleasant. But I see a deep frown and a disturbed look on the face of one man. His overcoat is ratty; his hair is matted with lint specks in it; his beard is like steel wool. This man is not one of our regular guests.

"Here comes Mr. Trouble," warns Jacee. I nod.

Brother Pace begins, "Let us bow our heads in reverence to God. Thank you, Heavenly Father, for this day and for this food. Please bless this food, those who prepared it, and those who are about to receive it. In Jesus' name we pray. Amen." As our guests begin to eat; we busy ourselves replenishing butter, bread, pitchers of juice and the like. Suddenly, we hear a loud snarl.

"Get your nasty self away from me!" I look at the source. It's Mr. Trouble, who has crazy eyes and spit in his beard.

"Hey, man, you can't sit at this end of the table all by yourself! There's four empty seats and four plates of food down here. You have your food, so what's your problem?" A small, but determined-looking man is facing Mr. Trouble. He's not aggressive, yet he's not backing down. Most of the people keep on eating and asking for seconds. Jacee scoots behind the food counter. Brother Pace alerts Brother Sampson and walks carefully with him up to the two men. I move slowly toward the back door because I see Mr. Trouble reach his hand down in his pocket. A knife appears in that hand. It looks like a small pocket knife, but it has a pointed tip that could do damage. Brother Sampson, who is also a Trenton police officer, takes over.

"Cut this mess out! We are not about to have fighting in this church annex!" His voice is like thunder and his right hand is on a holstered semiautomatic. His steely eyes demand attention. At over six feet tall and at least two hundred seventy-five pounds, Officer Sampson is an impressive figure.

"Place that knife down on the table and put your hands on your head, Jim. You know I don't play. Don't make me shoot you in the name of the Lord." Officer Brother Sampson directs a dangerous smile at Jim. Brother Pace stands next to the other guy, looking ready for action. Jim quickly follows Officer Sampson's directions and is led out of the building. He won't be allowed to return; that's our policy. Peace is a prerequisite. Thank God we have security during these feedings, because people sometimes do get out of hand. One would think they'd be so content with the free food, clothing, and services that fighting would be the last thing on their minds. But, some of them have mental and emotional issues, so we have an outburst like Jim's every now and then.

Jacee rushes over. "NikkiMac, I saw you sliding over to the back door. Was that a crazy scene, or what?"

"I don't know how you managed to catch a glimpse of me, since you were flying behind the counter! I was just getting out of harm's way, and I'm not ashamed of it!" We both laugh.

"You shouldn't be ashamed of it, Sister NikkiMac. Those who get out of the way live to see another day." Brother Pace grins broadly. "The smaller guy's name is Bill. I told him the next time someone starts trouble with him here, he needs to tell one of the brothers and not try to solve it himself. That's why we have our brother Officer Sampson here. All we need is for a fight to break out and for someone to get hurt. That would make our benevolent effort look bad. Most of our guests are peaceful and thankful, but you do get a few bad apples sometimes."

From the front door comes a loud, cheerful greeting. "Jacee and NikkiMac! Hey y'all!" It's Angeleese, one of our regulars. She and her five little stair-step children show up faithfully each month. She's no bigger than a minute, but it seems she's been popping out babies every nine months for the past few years. When I first met her, she said she was mixed. I didn't ask her to explain. I assumed she meant: one Black parent and one White parent. She's got curly, dark brown hair, a creamy skin tone, and a petite, shapely body. Her full, pink lips cover bright, tiny teeth. At first glance, she fools you, but within three minutes of a conversation you realize she's slow mentally. Nevertheless, Angeleese is a happy, friendly, affectionate soul who keeps looking for love. The problem is because she's a person with intellectual disabilities, at least four different men have conned her, impregnated her, and kept on stepping. Angeleese starts her ritual of cheerfully and repeatedly introducing the children to anyone who pauses and greets her.

"This is my big boy, Scooter. He six. His daddy name is Ron." Scooter's saucer-like eyes are set under bushy black eyebrows. He shows a slow smile, exposing a wide gap between his two upper front teeth. He frequently darts the tip of his pink tongue in and out of his gap.

"This is my smart girl, Ziggy. She five. Her daddy name is Bill." Ziggy is short and fat, like a beach ball with feet, arms, a head, and almost no neck. Everything about her is round.

"Hello, my name is Ziggy and I am five years old. I go to school. My teacher's name is Miss Boston."

"Cha-Cha four. Her daddy dead. He got runned over by a car." Cha-Cha moves constantly, yet she never leaves her mother's side. She's all snapping fingers and shuffling feet. Her little head bops up and down while her eyes blink rapidly.

"This Mookie and Shay Shay. They twins. They both three. Cletus is they daddy, even though he say he not." The twins Mookie and Shay Shay hold hands and stare. They are so cute, but the lights in their eyes aren't on. Their pigeon-toed feet turn inward and their high behinds toot outward.

I like Angeleese, but I feel sorry for her. I want to slap the men who got her pregnant, because she doesn't know any better. She just wants love. Chronologically, she's 25 years old, but in terms of her thinking and emotional skills, she's more a like twelve year old. She, her elderly grandmother, and her children live in a subsidized apartment near the church building. She's a sweet soul who bothers no one; she loves her babies. Those doggy men who take advantage of her gullible nature and need for affection need to be shot. To me, what they do to her is like taking advantage of a child.

"Hello, Miss Angeleese. Hello, children; it's good to see all of you." Jacee and I wave to them.

"You know I come every feeding Saturday. I got to feed these five crumb crushers of mine, and get some more clothes for us. God bless you all at this church for helping out."

Jacee blurts, "Angeleese, why don't you make these babies' fathers pay child support? It would help you take care of your children's needs. I know you probably get some public assistance, but these men owe the children at least financial support, even if they don't try to stay in their lives!"

I touch Jacee's arm to back her up; I don't want her to hurt Angeleese's feelings. Of course, Jacee rolls her eyes at me, but she does stop talking. Angeleese smiles sweetly, and then responds, "Jacee, I hear what you say, but I gotta do things my way. I don't want the agency people all up in my business. Besides, some of they daddies give me money when they can. But not Cha-Cha's; he can't pay from his grave. It's alright; we make out okay." Then, Angeleese marches her line of children past us and toward a table. They make me think of a mother duck leading her ducklings to the pond for a swim. She calls back to me, "Just pray for me and my babies, NikkiMac. Okay?" I promise her that I will do that.

Now, Jacee looks apologetic. "NikkiMac, thank you for shutting me up because I didn't mean to offend Angeleese. I really don't ever want to hurt her feelings. She's one of the sweetest people I know. But why does it seem like so many people with mental disabilities are slow about everything else except romance?"

"I hear you, Jacee. Of all the adult ones I know, their physical attraction drive seems to be intact, even overactive. Remember Lizella and Hector? They used to attend church here awhile ago. Lizella was definitely special, and she zeroed in on Hector from the get-go. Hector had intellectual disabilities too, but he was more functional than Lizella. She followed him around the church, smiling and trying to hold his hand. At first, he seemed okay with the attention, but then I think he got scared with her always grinning her buck-toothed smile at him. Lizella's stern guardian used to drop her off and pick her up after service; she never spoke to us and she did not like to wait for Lizella. I think Hector walked to church and got a ride home on the church van. I believe they both got baptized, but there was some controversy about whether or not they understood what they were doing."

"Oh, that's right. I remember them. So, NikkiMac, did they ever hook up?"

"There wasn't much chance of it, since they saw each other only at church. However, one Sunday, I saw Lizella corner Hector at the back of the church, push him against the wall, and ask him for a kiss. She was all up in his face, blocking out his sunlight, and puckering her lips as much as her protruding teeth would allow. I thought he was going to faint!"

"I know that's right! Did they kiss?"

"No, I stepped in by calling her name, and telling her that her guardian had arrived to drive her home from church. That announcement got her swiftly away from poor Hector. Lizella wanted that kiss, but not badly enough to make her strict guardian come in the building and get loud on her for making her wait."

We laugh and get back to work filling pitchers with juice. I wave at Angeleese and her children. They almost fill up a table. All six of them manage to wave back without missing a chew of food. All of our guests eat, some socialize, some request spiritual counseling. Some check out the Clothing Bank. Then, they take their bags and leave the building. They wander down the street; they are back out in their world. Most of the crowd moves through by 3 o'clock. As we start to clean off the tables, I see a blur rush past me.

"Hey, NikkiMac! I didn't know you were working today or I woulda come here sooner for my vittles!" Cletus, his hands full of empty plastic bags, is here to collect leftovers. Trailing right behind him is stank crack head Tasha. She grins and her bad lip paint job makes her look like a clown. Her surprised eye focuses on me; I don't know who or what her other eye views.

"What's up, NikkiMac? Are me and Cletus too late for food? We may not be holy, but we sure are two hungry souls." She snickers at her joke. She makes me want to spit. I don't respond to her.

"Cletus and Tasha, if you'll come over to table number ten; I'll pack up some food for you." Brother Pace's voice sounds gentle and calm.

"Jacee, how can she bring her raggedy-looking self in here and embarrass her father like that? She's just trying to make him look bad because he put her out of his home. What a tramp!"

"Calm yourself, NikkiMac. You sound like me, all indignant. Brother Pace has it under control." I look at his face, and it appears he does. He helps Cletus and Tasha pack up their plastic bags and even tosses in some extra packages of rolls. I guess that's the Christ-like spirit our minister is always preaching about. After we close up for the day, I walk out to the parking lot with Brother Pace.

"Please tell me, how were you able to deal so peacefully with your daughter Tasha at the feeding today?"

"I love her, NikkiMac. I don't love her lifestyle. If it weren't for the Holy Spirit, I would be hostile towards Tasha, because she betrays the way she was raised by me and the late Sister Pace. I hate the behavior, but showing agape love means that with God's help, I can love the unlovable. I can seek their highest good. After all, God loves me even when I sin. God loves all of us, and wants what's best for His children. I want Tasha to return to God. She was added to the kingdom when she was in her teens, but she strayed away when she was in her twenties. Alcohol and drugs lured her away from God and into a worldly lifestyle. She made the choice at first, now the drugs make choices for her. No, I don't want her to live with me, but I keep her life insurance paid up, I keep her in prayer, and I help her in the wisest way I know how."

"I hear what you're saying, Brother Pace, but I truly need growth in this area of dealing lovingly with people who get on my nerves. I know this much, if you were my father, I would be proud to show you love and respect. You are a good Christian man."

"Sister NikkiMac, I believe God sent me your way years ago in that Club Taste parking lot. You needed help with Darius Muse, but more importantly, you needed to seek God for direction in your life. I praise God that you are serious about your Christian walk. You often come to me for advice from the scriptures, and I notice the way you try to look out for me. I'm so proud of the way you have hung in there and stayed with the Lord."

"Brother Pace, you have been like a guardian angel to me since I met you."

"You are my sister in Christ, but it's more than that. I feel like you are family. I think of you as my church daughter. Is that okay with you?"

My eyes tear, my lower lip quivers, and my heart feels full. "I'd consider it an honor to be your church daughter."

"Then it's official. You'll call me Poppa Pace and I'll call you Daughter NikkiMac." He embraces me with the most loving, honest, caring, protective, paternal hug I've received in my grownup years.

My oh my, Poppa Pace gives great hugs.

Chapter 10   Scents, Sense, and Sensibility

As we reach the close of *Holy, Holy, Holy*, the opening hymn, I get a whiff of stale corn chips. Jacee and I involuntarily wrinkle up our noses and look at each other with quizzical expressions. I know from past experience that this type of odor comes from the actual corn chips, from sweaty fake leather shoes, or from a dirty curly perm. To my left is a 60-ish female visitor who is using a hand fan to cool herself. Maybe she's having a hot flash. The fanning motion pushes the scent in my direction big time. I purposely sniff; it's her hair that I smell. Jacee hands me a note that reads, "She got that *Forever Girl Curl*: forever she been wearing it, and she sho nuff a girl!" Jacee is two kinds of crazy. I struggle hard not to laugh at her attempt to write using country dialect, but I fail and try to cover my laughter with a phony cough. Usher Gray walks past our pew and frowns, but we act like we don't see him.

Sometimes, our people get these curly perms and go for weeks without washing their hair. They just keep spraying the dirty hair and sweaty scalp with curl activator. They delay washing it, because the hair takes three days to a week to get saturated enough to look shiny and moist again. Wearers find the hair style convenient. They think it makes their hair grow, and it won't sweat out like a press and curl. It will, however, ruin pillowcases and any other surface you rest your head against. Some make their curly perm last up to three months without getting a touch-up of the new growth. Others make it go longer; they spray, pick, and pat their hair daily for six months or so. They think the hair looks fly, but others think it's a wet, funky, hot mess. This type of wet curly perm has mostly gone out of style here in Trenton but there are some diehards who won't let it go. There's nothing wrong with that; they just need to maintain the style properly. Our visitor is the curly perm offender, but she's come to hear the gospel. I breathe shallowly, shift slightly, and continue singing. Jacee crosses her eyes at me; then she settles down.

Brother Johnson's sermon is entitled, *Escape Your Fears: Change is Inevitable*. I write the title in my notes and prepare to learn something.

"Christians, God does not want us to be fearful people. Don't be fearful of circumstances, change, finances, relationships, challenges, danger, or even death. We don't have to fear anything because we belong to God and we are under His divine protection. Turn in your Bibles to the book of Revelation; the last book in the New Testament. Find chapter 1, verses 9 through 20. Let us together read the account of the Apostle John, which was written while he was exiled on the island of Patmos. Here he was spoken to by Jesus. Focus on verse 17; Jesus told him to be unafraid. Christians, that message is also for us today! Turn to Genesis chapter 26, verse 24. God knew all about Isaac's trying situation and told Isaac not to be afraid. In Genesis chapter 46, verse 3, God told Jacob not to be afraid to go to Egypt because He would be with Jacob. As our young people would say, God had Jacob's back! In Exodus chapter 14, verse 14, Moses told the Israelites who were fleeing from Egypt's pharaoh that the Lord would fight for them. This is the God we serve, Christians. Practice the presence of Him everywhere you go. If you do this, regardless of any change or situation you face, you won't be overcome by fear."

Brother Johnson has my attention because I sometimes become fearful about circumstances that are out of my control. I have a pattern of working hard at being prepared for whatever may happen. I become apprehensive when all my careful preparation is ineffective because the situation is one over which I have no power.

"Here are some points for you to consider; write them in your notes and reflect on them in your daily quiet time with God. We should all make some daily time for God, isn't that right, church?"

"That's right!"

"Amen!"

"Develop the habit of accepting change. Realize that life itself is the story of change; our human state is fluid. Fear does not make change come to a halt. Learn to adapt to the unavoidable and to make the most of every situation."

"Amen! Amen!" More brothers sign off on the preacher's point.

"Develop the habit of complete trust in God and you will silence fear. Fear robs you of your joy and peace. God will never let you down. Can I get a witness that God has never let you down?"

"Say so, Preacher!"

"Glory to God!"

After completing his message, Brother Johnson issues the invitation, "Is there anyone here this afternoon who wants to be added to God's kingdom? Come and be baptized into Christ. Have your sins forgiven. Receive the Holy Spirit, and enjoy the guidance and protection of God. Live faithfully until death and heaven will be your forever home."

We stand and Brother Vonner starts singing *Just As I Am*. On the third note, a shrill cry assaults the atmosphere.

"No, please don't sing that song. It reminds me of my dead mother! It was her favorite church song!"

All eyes turn to Sister Pipps, a very neurotic woman who, when she does attend, sits on the second pew and twitches throughout the service. Some say that she refuses to take her medications on a regular basis. I guess she's harmless, but she rarely talks and she dresses like she's going to a secondhand ball. She often wears dated cocktail dresses topped with little fur capes and pumps with rundown heels. Judging by her loud outcry, she clearly feels like talking today, but Brother Vonner is not having any of this.

"Like I was saying before the interruption, we'll sing all five verses of *Just As I Am*, and he starts leading the song. We follow him, except for frazzled Sister Pipps, who proceeds to howl, get up from her seat, and place her body flat out on the floor in front of the communion table.

"Oh no, don't sing that song!" she wails. Sister Pipps begins to rotate in the aisle. She keeps most of her body stiff and somehow manages to roll from the side of one aisle to the side of the other aisle. Her body position brings to mind the childhood fun of rolling down the grassy hills at Trenton's famed Cadwalader Park: arms stretched straight overhead and legs twirling. Sister Pipps continues to cry out in protest about us singing the hymn. Some of us look stunned, others giggle, and others wear expressions of extreme disapproval. Then, Ushers Gray and Dexter spring into action. They approach Sister Pipps and gently try to lift her up. Unfortunately, she's wearing a short fluffy party dress. On her way up from the floor, we see too much information from underneath the dress.

The ushers don't miss a beat, and in short order, Sister Pipps is whisked from the room. I notice that Sister Sharlette is right behind the three of them; she's always ready to assist when a woman's touch is needed.

Even though the show's over before we finish singing verse three of the hymn, we continue through all five verses. I learn two unexpected things today: the ushers can be useful as well as ornamental, and when Brother Vonner says we're going to sing all five verses of a hymn, he means it.

Chapter 11 Adam Greene and Sagging Jeans

Brother Johnson is introducing a new member to the congregation. His name is Adam Greene; he has a degree in ministry from a southern Christian college.

"Dear members, Brother Greene has been worshipping with the church in Huntsville, Alabama, but his job has relocated him to Trenton. He wants to place his membership here. I've just read to you his letter of recommendation from his former pastor in Huntsville. It's always a joy for me to receive a glowing report about a Christian who wants to place membership with us. It is wise to have a letter sent from the leadership of the former congregation, because some people are not in good standing where they came from. Sometimes, these troublesome and unfaithful members of the church stay long enough to cause problems at one congregation, and then they bounce to another congregation. We need to be aware of this. According to his former minister and elders, Brother Greene taught Bible classes and did pulpit preaching. We are blessed to receive him. Oh, this is for the eligible sisters; Brother Greene is in his late forties. He's an engineer by trade; a widower with no children. Now you know!" I hear soft chuckles.

Sister Batts, who is always looking for a man, utters, "I heard that!" I certainly feel blessed, but not just because of his glowing report; Adam Greene is fine! I attempt to appear cool, but looking at him makes my salivary glands activate. They squirt mouth liquid like when I bite into a sweet fruit first thing in the morning. What is my problem? I have seen good-looking men about my age before, but not this handsome, and certainly not in church. The outside of my left thigh is burning from Jacee's jabbing fist. She must feel the same burn because I am repeatedly pounding the outside of her right thigh. Brother Adam Greene is all that and a bag of chips!

"Members, please give Brother Greene the right hand of fellowship before you leave today. Greet him with the warmth that our Trenton congregation is known for."

The congregation says, "Amen!" I think the single women say it the loudest. Service continues. After communion, teenager Brother Antron Baker walks down the middle aisle, and some heads nod from side to side in disapproval. The top of his blue jeans are nestled underneath his small butt cheeks, which are covered with a black knit shirt. His underwear can't be seen, but the shape of his rear end certainly can. His gleaming white sneakers are untied, with the tongues pulled out and up. He walks in a clipped fashion because the way he's wearing the pants limits his stride. Young Antron is representing the "sagging" style to the maximum. He's been changing this past year. He used to hang out with the church children and wear suits and dress shoes to church. Sometimes the suits and shoes looked oversized, but he did look like a young man who put effort into dressing for church. He used to be shy and pleasant. Now he is frequently sullen and attitudinal.

"We may be losing him," I whisper to Jacee.

"You know, NikkiMac, I think I saw him this past week, hanging out with some thuggish guys. They appeared to be older than him; I think he's about thirteen years old now."

"Sister Arpaige Baker, his mom, still attends church services, but their interaction appears strained. I saw them having a heated conversation as they walked home from here last Sunday. I pulled my car over and offered them a ride, but Sister Arpaige declined. Antron just kept walking ahead of her. I don't know, Jacee. Maybe I should ask Brother Pace to speak with the young brother. Brother Pace interacts well with the young people here. He takes time with them; they know he understands and listens to them. That boy needs a positive Christian man's direct influence. I'll be right back; I drank a bottle of water on the way here, so you know where I'm headed. Jacee chuckles and lets me pass so I can handle my business. On my way back from the restroom, I see Usher Gray confront young Antron in the lobby outside the auditorium. Of course, I stop, look, and listen. It's what I do.

"Boy, you are supposed to be a Christian. Pull those pants up like you've got some good sense. You are disrespecting yourself and the church assembly, coming here looking like a gangster. Don't you know you are in church? It's bad enough for a Christian to dress like that anywhere, but you come to church like that?"

"Man, I have to go to the bathroom. Get out of my face. Why you sweatin' me? You don't buy my clothes!" Antron stares up at the usher's face. The teenager's thin frame is rigid; his arms are taut at his sides. His hands are in tight fists.

"Boy, who do you think you're giving backtalk to?" Usher Gray looks like he's about to lay down his religion. Just then, Sister Arpaige bursts through the doors from the auditorium.

"What's going on? What's wrong, Antron?" She walks over to her son.

"All I did was tell him to pull his pants up, and he wants to get all smart with me. Why did you let him come here dressed like a hoodlum?" Usher Gray is not in the mood to back down, and neither is Sister Baker. She is pissed, and I'm wondering how long they're going to ignore the Holy Spirit.

"Brother Gray, this is my son, not yours. If you have something to say to him, run it by me first. Besides, the way he dresses is none of your business. Do you think because you have a little usher pin on your lapel that you're the church police? I hope not, because as far as I know, the Bible doesn't say anything about ushers, much less ushers patrolling the congregation!" Usher Gray's eyes look like they are about to pop out of his head. His big chest rises as he takes a deep breath and opens his mouth to reply. Just then, Brother Pace appears and brings with him a cool breeze of peace.

"Christians, Christians, calm down, please." His voice is warm; not confrontational. Antron looks at Brother Pace. The teenager's face softens.

"Come here, son. You too, Mom. Let's go into the conference room and sort this out. Brother Gray, would you join us please? We are all Christians, we are in God's house, and He loves us." Brother Pace's arm rests around the teenager's shoulder; his hand is on Sister Baker's elbow. Calmly, they begin to walk with him.

Usher Gray stands still. "I'm on duty here, Brother Pace, I can't leave my post. I'll tell you what happened later."

Brother Pace stops, looks back over his shoulder, and replies, "Okay, brother, I'm going to hold you to that."

I return to my seat. The congregation is singing *Leaning On The Everlasting Arms*. Minister Johnson approaches the pulpit. "I'm pleased to have some visitors' cards. We don't want to embarrass you, and you don't have to speak, but please stand or raise your hand so we can recognize and greet you before you leave today." He begins announcing our visitors. Young Antron and his mother enter the auditorium. The teenager's pants are waist up, his shirt tail is tucked in, and he walks unhampered. Sister Baker seems composed as she and her son sit together. I don't see Brother Pace, but I know that he, with God's help, made this peace happen. That's the type of faithful man he is.

After service, the congregation gathers in the aisles, the lobby, outside on the grassy areas, on the steps, and in the parking lot. It's time to shake hands with each other and enjoy fellowship. For the most part, we are a very social and warm group. The sounds of laughter and conversation are lively. Of course, the children feel finally free, so they run all over the grounds. We constantly have to make sure we don't bump them with our cars as we drive out of the parking lot.

I spot my Poppa Pace and Usher Gray talking peacefully on the church steps. They shake hands, give each other shoulder hugs, and part. Then, my attention goes to Brother Adam Greene. His smile looks super white because his skin is so dark and chocolaty. Three or four sisters buzz around him; he graciously tries to give them individual eye contact and responses. Sister Melody is one of the admiring women. She's cheesing so hard that her teeth look like they're about to pop out of her mouth. I've never seen such a big smile on an actual person. It resembles a cartoon character smile: ear to ear, like a cob of fresh Jersey corn. She supposedly has a man, so I wonder why she is all up in Brother Greene's face.

"Brother Greene, how would you like a down home southern style dinner? I'm known for my mouth-watering meals, made from scratch. I don't believe in cooking from out of a box or just throwing food in a microwave. Are you available to come over for dinner one night this week?" Sister Melody is laying it on thick. Adam smiles and gets ready to respond when Sister Carolina waddles closer to him, and her hips nudge Sister Melody over about a foot. Melody stops smiling and slowly sashays away from Adam, calling out, "I'll talk to you later, Brother Greene. Think about a date for our meal." Sister Melody gives way to the ample hips of Sister Carolina.

"Brother Greene, I would not be so forward as to ask you, a single brother, to come to my home for an evening dinner. We both know that it would be on the up-and-up, but some people might start wagging their tongues about it being inappropriate. The Bible tells us to be hospitable, but it also tells us not to cause our good deeds be spoken of in a bad way. That's why I want to offer you a food basket from my kitchen. You need to taste my chicken and dumplings, so good they'll make a rabbit hug a hound! I can bring your meal to church next Sunday, and you can take it home and enjoy a dinner prepared with Christian love." Sister Carolina smiles ever so sweetly at Brother Greene.

The twins, Sister Lelah Maze and Sister Lolah Maze, simply smile at Adam and repeat, "We are so glad you have come our way. We are looking forward to your preaching, Brother Greene." Actually, Lolah does the talking; her sister Lelah does the grinning.

Brother Adam takes this all in. He's gentle in his responses. His green eyes are mesmerizing, yet they carry a hint of some private pain. He has an air of purpose and strength, yet looks like he could appreciate a safe hug every now and then. As the sisters vie for his attention, he shifts his weight from one of his lean, slightly bowed legs to the other. Adam's height must be about six feet, two inches. The old folks would say, "He's a tall drink of water." His shoes look to be about a size thirteen. His fingers are long and his hands are big. I remember the saying about men who have large hands and feet. Then I catch myself, because sinful and passionate thoughts are waiting at my mind's door. My feet move me away from the scene as I try to out walk my fleshly thoughts.

"Hello Daughter NikkiMac. How are you today? I didn't get a chance to greet you before service this morning. Where's my hug?"

"Poppa Pace, I saw you earlier, but you were dealing with Usher Gray and young Antron." I rush into his protective arms for my hug. It's the best contact I've had today.

"Yeah, sometimes it's not so much what a person says as the way a person says it. The way we talk to each other is important."

"But Poppa Pace, Brother Gray should know that he can't talk to people, especially fellow Christians, like he's arguing with them. That's just common sense."

"Daughter NikkiMac, common sense is not always common." It takes me a minute to wrap my mind around his statement; but I realize it is true. Lots of people fail to use common sense in dealing with others.

"Poppa Pace, how did you get Brother Gray to settle down this morning? It looked like he was about to get real funky with Sister Arpaige and Antron."

"I just reasoned with him from the scriptures, Daughter NikkiMac. Jesus speaks about how we should interact with one another in Matthew chapter 7, verse 12. Some people call this *The Golden Rule*, but Jesus didn't announce it as such, so I don't. Anyway, His message is for us to treat others the way we want to be treated. I don't want anyone getting smart with me or insulting me, so I shouldn't give that behavior out to anyone. One may not want to listen to another person, but Christians worth the salt that goes in their bread will listen to what Jesus says. That's what happened with Brother Gray; he needed to put himself in the shoes of Brother Antron and Sister Arpaige. How would he have liked to be addressed? I don't think he means any harm; he just needs help in learning how to interact with others. I plan to talk more with Brother Gray as well as ask our minister to speak to him about showing Christ-like behavior. That should help. Brother Gray did apologize to Antron and his mother, which shows some progress. They accepted his apology and offered one to him for their part in the situation."

"I hear what you're saying, Poppa Pace, but why did the leadership appoint Brother Gray to be one of our ushers when he doesn't know how to talk to people? That seems wrong."

"I'm not sure, but I plan to speak with Brother Johnson. Maybe the brother who heads the group of ushers thinks Brother Gray should have a chance to become more involved in the congregation. We'll work it out; don't you worry. In the meantime, pray for Brother Gray, because that's the right thing for you to do."

My first thought is not in agreement with praying for Brother Gray, but then I have a second thought and reply, "I'll try, Poppa Pace."

Chapter 12   Pray for Me

"Good morning, brothers, sisters, and visitors. We are about to begin our morning worship service. Before the reading of scripture, are there any prayer requests?" Brother Flowers pauses and looks over the congregation.

Brother Sills arises quickly and clears his throat before speaking. "I'd like to ask for prayer, Brother Flowers. I have sinned in that I have not been attending worship services on a regular basis. I am without excuse, because I am never absent from my job. Of course, I hold a very important and demanding position that no one else at my workplace can handle, so I have to be there. Still, I realize that I should be more faithful in my church attendance. Anyway, I would like for a faithful brother, like our minister, to pray for me. I don't need an unfaithful brother to pray for me, only a faithful one."

"Oh no, he did not!" Jacee is in my ear. "He's the one in need of and asking for prayer! How is he going to select someone to pray for him?" I am about to assume *The Position*, because Brother Sills is showing us all that he has more nerve than sense. Then I hear Brother Flowers, our older brother who used to be a lot more outspoken when members strayed away from doctrine, but he's gotten quieter this past couple of years. He speaks slowly, precisely, and gently.

"Brother Sills, your request for prayer has been heard, but you don't indicate repentance of your sin. What you do express is the fact about faithful attendance. You're right, Hebrews chapter 10, verse 25 addresses that. You say that you're indispensable at your job; are you aware that you would not have a job if God had not so blessed you? Are you also aware that you display a judgmental spirit by implying that our minister is the only brother here that is faithful enough to pray for you?"

The congregation says "Amen." It appears that the old Brother Flowers has shown up today!

At first, Brother Sills looks at Brother Flowers and is quiet. Then, he speaks to us. "Dear congregation, Brother Flowers is correct. I just showed the wrong attitude. I repent and ask for your forgiveness. I also ask for God's forgiveness."

He sits down and we say "Amen" again. We bow our heads as Brother Flowers says the prayer. He's followed by Brother Carlos, who does the scripture reading. Carlos may be silly and playful when he's not performing a role in service, but he's usually quite serious when he serves in the worship.

After the scripture reading, Brother Vonner leads us in song. We then have communion, and service is peaceful and spiritual. Minister Johnson's name is announced; he walks toward the pulpit while we sing the last verse of *I Love My Savior, Too*. The brothers pump up their a cappella bass line; they are robustly singing to the Lord. It makes my heart feel full, and I race to keep up with the alto part.

Brother Pace intercepts Minister Johnson just before the preacher steps into the pulpit. Bro. Pace whispers in Minister Johnson's ear. The minister nods his head, then steps to the microphone and speaks, "Brothers, sisters, and visiting friends, please excuse the interruption, but I ask that Brother Vonner lead two more hymns before I begin today's sermon. I'm going into the lobby with Brother Sampson. We need to assist Sister Longstreet with an emergency situation. Please continue to praise the Lord in song." We sing as Brother Johnson and Brother Sampson walk up the center aisle toward the lobby.

I look at Jacee and whisper, "Jacee, what do you think is going on? Sister Longstreet was baptized about a month ago, remember? Every time she attended here she was with a little popeyed man. He was so glued to her side that I assumed he was her boyfriend. He kept rolling his eyes at any man who looked her way. He even rolled his eyes at old Brother Kelsey, and I think he's ninety years old! Well, after about four Sundays, she accepted the gospel and was baptized. The boyfriend didn't seem to be happy about it, either."

"NikkiMac, I heard they were living together and the boyfriend got mad when she moved out of his place. He thinks she's being brainwashed by the church. You know how some worldly men are; he's probably freaking because she's no longer under his control."

"Shh! Stop whispering and sing, you sinners!" Brother Carlos messes with us. We do stop talking, though, because Carlos is right. Just as we finish the last verse of *Give Me The Bible*, Brother Johnson enters the room and goes to the pulpit. Sister Longstreet and Brother Sampson enter the auditorium and take their seats. She looks relieved.

Brother Johnson begins. "Church, when one of us hurts, we all hurt. Our Sister Longstreet has a situation that I am going to mention here; she has asked me to do so. When she was recently added to the church and learned more about what God says, she decided to move out of her former boyfriend's home. She believes what the Bible says about marriage being honorable. She now realizes that living romantically with a man outside of the marriage bond violates God's will. Our sister informed this man that since she is now letting God direct her steps, their entire relationship must change. Unfortunately, he did not like this and is dangerously angry about her decision. He has threatened her more than once. Today, he was waiting outside to talk to her, but he left. Thankfully, Brother Pace knew a little about this situation and recognized this man, so he told Sister Longstreet and she asked for our assistance. Understandably, she does not want to interact with this man right now. She has moved into the family home of one of our church members and is in the process of obtaining a restraining order. For added security, she wants her church family to be aware in case this man shows up around here. His name is Butch Mathers. Unless he shows a change of heart and comes to hear the gospel, he has no business here, stalking our sister. Let one of the brothers, especially Brother Sampson, know if you see him on or near our church grounds. Meanwhile, please embrace Sister Longstreet. She's just a babe in Christ, yet she's allowing the Holy Spirit to help her be obedient to God's will, even under duress. Church, let's sing one more song before I preach today's sermon. Don't worry; it won't be my regular length because I know I'm starting thirty minutes later than I usually do. Actually, Sister Longstreet has demonstrated my message for today. You'll see when I begin. Right now I think we need to talk to Him in song."

"Amen, brother!"

"Yes, Lord!"

The words and harmony of *Just A Little Talk With Jesus* fill the auditorium as we speak to the Lord and to each other in song.

Chapter 13   Seat Ownership Issues

Brother Sanders steps into the pulpit to lead us in prayer, so I slip out of my designer shoes, because I know we're going to be standing up for a long time. These heels are four inches high, and I don't want my toes to be barking. One time, Jacee clocked Brother Sanders at seven minutes for a congregational prayer. "Brother Pray So Long" is what I call him; and I do so with affection. He's a nice brother and really sincere, but in prayer, he is longwinded. In turn, he playfully teases me about my big singing voice. "Sister NikkiMac Megaphone" is what he calls me. It's all good, as the kids say, because there's no ill will involved. After Brother Sanders finishes praying, the congregation sits, and the ushers open the double doors to allow the latecomers into the auditorium. The way some people behave about their church seats is funny to me.

"Jacee, check this out. The usher is about to bring people in and there's plenty of free space on the pew where Sister Sadie is sitting. I bet that's where he's leading them. She doesn't seem to mind if they sit down, but she's not going to move much. You know she thinks that's her special seat on the pew."

"I know, NikkiMac, here we go!" Jacee is always ready for a show. Usher Dexter walks to elderly Sister Sadie and asks her to move down because he needs to seat four people. She frowns and moves over just enough to accommodate maybe two people. The four people come in and squash themselves into a space suitable for two. Sister Sadie acts as if she doesn't notice the squeeze. The squashed people look at her like she's nuts. I often wonder why some people hate to let latecomers sit. Why do they move down grudgingly and just barely? It's like they own that spot and dare anyone to move them from it. If some could, I believe they'd put nameplates on the seats to mark them.

Nice Brother Dexter persists. "Sister Sadie, could you please move down a little more?" He says it so softly and politely. Sister Sadie responds through her false teeth that slip up and down while she speaks.

"Why do I have to move? I got here on time and I always get to my seat!" But she does move. With much attitude, she grabs her purse, Bible, walking stick, and makes room for the squeezed people.

"Thank you, Sister Sadie. God bless." Usher Dexter smiles at her. She sneers back at him. The four people spread out so they can be comfortable. They send a look of gratitude to Usher Dexter. They try not to look at Sister Sadie; maybe they're afraid to further rile the old woman. Sister Sadie directs her words at Usher Dexter.

"You had better be glad I'm trying to get my old self to heaven, or I would fight you about this! People need to get to church on time!" Usher Dexter doesn't break his smile. He's so tactful. Maybe his tact will rub off on Usher Gray someday. We sing the last verse of *Sweeter As The Years Go By*, and then we get quiet for the scripture reading by Brother Cliff.

"Please turn in your Bibles to Psalm 1." The familiar sound of shuffling pages is heard. He reads aloud and we follow along reading silently in our Bibles. It's a serious thing in the church for members to bring their own Bibles to classes and worship services. We are encouraged to see for ourselves what the Bible says, not to simply listen and accept what the preacher says, without any biblical investigation. My Bible, like most I've seen of my fellow members', is marked with pen and highlighter, sticky notes, and such. Passages and verses that are most helpful are marked for my easy reference.

A not-so-soft, choppy, guttural sound punctuates Brother Cliff's reading. I see a few questioning glances. Brother Cliff continues; the noise continues and even escalates. It sounds like someone gargling in a bathroom. Brother Cliff finishes reading and asks, "Would someone gently shake Brother Kelsey awake before we begin the prayer?" The old man's chin rests on his left shoulder. His eyes are closed. Brother Kelsey is one of the first members here on Sundays, but he goes to sleep at the same time, right after communion. You can tell time by Brother Kelsey's first nod and snore at 11:30 on Sunday morning. Maybe the sleepiness is caused by his medication, or something in the grape juice we use for communion. It might just be the fact that he's so old. One thing's for certain, he never drops his Bible when he's sleeping. I have never seen that happen.

Usher Gray softly taps Brother Kelsey's shoulder; the senior citizen's eyelids flutter and his eyes open wide. He lifts his Bible to show the usher. "Thank you, good brother. I'm fine, thank you."

After prayer, we sing *I'll Live in Glory* and *Master, The Tempest Is Raging*. Then, to my surprise, Brother Adam Greene walks to the pulpit with Minister Johnson. "Christian family and visitors, we are in for a gospel treat. This is the fifth Sunday, so you know that following service, we'll gather in our dining hall after worship and share a delicious fellowship meal prepared by our Kitchen Committee. This time provides wonderful opportunities to interact with the persons you may not usually have a chance to speak with on Sundays. I encourage you to extend this to phone calls and other contacts throughout the week. We are a family, so each of us needs to grow closer with as many of our sisters and brothers as possible. You can't love somebody well if you don't take the time to get to know them. During these fellowship meals, we have food for both our physical and social appetites. But first, we are going to receive a spiritual meal from our dear Brother Adam Greene."

"Amen," is the response from the congregation. Jacee and I elbow each other. Brother Johnson returns to his seat.

Brother Adam steps up to the microphone and issues a throaty, "Good morning, dear Christians and visitors. I appreciate having the privilege to share the word of God with you today. Let's first go to Him in prayer." He bows his head. "Our Father in heaven, holy is your name. Father, we thank you for life, your blessings, mercy, and grace. Be with us, Heavenly Father, as we go into your word. Help me as your speaker and all of us as listeners get the message you desire us to have for our spiritual growth. In Jesus' name we pray. Amen." We express our agreement and raise our heads. I reach for my notepad so I can take notes on the sermon.

"Please turn your in Bibles to Psalm 14; we are going to examine for a short while the mind of a fool. The Bible says that anyone who says there is no God is a fool. A fool is defined as one who is stupid, immoral, slow to understand, confused. Ezekiel chapter 18, verse 4 tells us that our souls belong to God. Who are we to decide there is no God when we are His creation and everything we have comes from Him? What we have from God is on loan to us; we don't own it. God is letting us borrow it. That jazzy car, the fine home, the good job, the stylish clothes- all are on loan to us from our Heavenly Father. Our material blessings are not to be worshipped. We should not let them become our idols. They are only things; they neither created us nor can they save us. When we define our own gods, we are acting as if we are God. Psalm 19, verse 1 speaks of the proof of God's existence and glory. Did you ever notice that God's other creations, like animals, the weather, and the waters, do what God tells them? Only His human creation attempts to have his own way and think for the Father. That's the mind of a fool!" Sister Hobson, who has recovered from being exposed by Brother Cliff about their joint fornication, stands up and waves her hands in the air.

"Hallelujah, Brother Greene, you better preach, man!" Since her repentance, she has been on fire for the Lord. She turns around in a circle and sits down. That's a good thing, too, because one of the ushers is headed her way. We are taught to have our services be orderly, less focused on emotion, and more focused on understanding and receiving God's word. That doesn't mean we can't express our agreement with the gospel, but we try not to distract from the message being preached. Well, most of us try, because our attention rightly belongs to God. Worship time is not show time.

"My friends, if we want to act the way we want, disregarding what God says, He will let us. Here's the catch: we are still accountable to God. So, let us trust Him and do what He tells us to do. He only tells us what is best for us; He knows us better than we know ourselves. I know what I plan to do. I plan to pay attention to God, so I will not have the mind of a fool. I urge you to do the same."

"Amen, brother!"

"I know that's right."

"Yes! Yes! Preach!"

"Praise the Lord!"

Brother Greene continues for a few more minutes and then wraps up the sermon with an invitation to any who want to come to Christ. We stand for the invitation song; it's *There Is Power In The Blood*. As we end verse one, Brother Greene steps from behind the pulpit and down from the platform. He begins to walk in the center aisle.

"If you have not been added through scriptural baptism into the kingdom of God, now is your time. I lovingly urge you to come forward as we continue to encourage you through song. I'll wait here for you to come. If you're shy, just raise your hand and I'll come to you. Members, if you see a visitor who might be making a move to come forward, take his or her hand and walk with that person." Brother Greene stretches out his arms in a welcoming gesture; we sing some more. My heart is so full from the sincerity of Adam's message that I do that throat-clutch move; it's like I'm crying in my throat. My eyes get moist, too. God has truly blessed this brother with the gift of preaching. One person walks down the aisle, then another, and a third.

"Amen! Amen!" says the congregation.

Brother Adam says, "Praise God." He smiles, hugs each person warmly, and then takes each person's confession. "I believe that Jesus Christ is the Son of God" is heard. Three consecutive baptisms are performed. The joyful feeling of three souls being saved envelopes the room. Brother Vonner wastes no time launching into *Salvation Has Been Brought Down*. Like Brother Sanders teases, I truly am "Sister NikkiMac Megaphone" as I blast my alto part, spurred on by the sweet soprano, full tenor, and pounding bass voices of fellow Christians. I am so glad that God gifted humans with pure vocal instruments. It's at moments like these that I deeply understand Colossians chapter 3, verse 16. What a spiritual charge!

Next, we have collection of and prayer for the weekly offering. Following that, Brother Martin steps up to the pulpit. "I will be reading the church announcements, but first, a reminder to the congregation to please greet our new members after service. Give them the right hand of fellowship. Also, kindly let our senior citizens go to the dining hall first and get seated for our meal today. Last time, poor Sister Blake almost got knocked down by people rushing to get food. There is plenty of food for everyone. Parents, grab hold of your children, because you know how after the dismissal prayer, they like to take off running. Some of them are always dashing around and bumping into folks."

I hear a sister say, "That sure is the truth; some of these parents need to watch their wild children."

"Brother Coles left his Sunday school book on his seat this morning and someone took it. Hopefully it was taken by mistake and not stolen. Amen?" Brother Martin pauses for effect as we affirm his remark.

"There are several letters here that announce meetings or programs to be held by neighboring congregations. I'm not going to read them because they will be posted on the church bulletin board; you can read them for yourself. Next, Brother Gray, one of our ushers, asks that members refrain from sitting in the seats near the double doors because they are designated for the ushers. That's why those seats have blue labeled covers on the seat backs. He says the ushers need to sit there in order to more efficiently perform their duties without stepping over folks in the pews."

My stomach growls so noisily that Jacee giggles. "Girl, you didn't eat breakfast this morning, did you?"

"No, Jacee. I overslept, so I skipped breakfast because I didn't want to be late for Sunday school. Maybe Brother Martin is almost finished with the dreaded announcements. I pretty much tuned him out after the first two; what did he say about Usher Gray?"

"Oh, Brother Gray wants people to stop sitting in those four labeled chairs by the doors because they are for ushers only."

"Why? There are only a few ushers. Most of the time, two or three of them are in the lobby during service. They have their own usher fellowship going on. The only ushers who sit in the chairs are Brother Dexter and Brother Sampson. Brother Gray is busy chatting, when he's not blocking folks from coming in the auditorium if they are late according to his clock."

Jacee smiles at me. "Remember when Brother Gray stood belly to belly with a beefy sister and blocked her from entering because we were one minute into the service? She simply backed up, came in the side door, and strolled right past him. He was visibly ticked off!"

"Yes, Jacee, I almost hollered! I think Brother Gray wanted to snatch her!" We notice that Brother Martin is now asking us to stand for closing prayer. Worship service is over, and I am starving, but Jacee and I greet other Christians, especially the three new converts. Brother Carlos approaches. He's not performing a church duty, so he's up to his craziness.

"Sisters NikkiMac and Jacee, are you staying for the meal?"

"Yes, Carlos, we're staying, but you probably aren't. You usually leave and come back for evening service. Why don't you hang out with us for the meal?"

"Sister NikkiMac, I used to stay when the church had more people who could cook working in the kitchen. The last time I stayed for a fellowship meal, I saw a very scary casserole. I prayed over it before I ate it, because it looked like it was moving."

"Carlos, you need to stop. There is nothing wrong with the food. Besides, the Kitchen Committee prepares only the main dishes. Church members contribute their specialty side dishes and desserts. There is always something tasty for everyone!" Jacee looks annoyed.

"It may be okay to you, Sister Jacee, but I can't eat just any kind of food."

"You know what, Carlos?" I offer, "Since you are so particular about your food, you need to hang with Sister Dallas Chestnut, because she prepares her own food for these meals. She brings her lunchbox, utensils, and her crazy self every time we have a fellowship meal. She says she doesn't eat any beef or pork, or any food on a plate that touches such meat or the juice from the meat. For example, she won't eat string beans seasoned with smoked ham hocks or bacon or neck bones. At one church dinner, she was served a plate of fried chicken, brown rice, and string beans. I watched her scrutinize it. At first, she smiled her approval. Then her eyebrows knitted together and her lips turned down at the corners. She looked like she smelled something foul. I watched as she pulled out a small piece of pink pork meat that was hiding out among the string beans. That sneaky meat could not hide from Sister Dallas! She pushed the plate away and refused to eat anything. I suggested that she eat the rice and chicken, but she felt the whole plate had been contaminated by the string bean juice tainted with pork." Jacee and Carlos crack up laughing at me.

"NikkiMac, you are two kinds of crazy!" howls Carlos. "That does not make any sense; you know you're lying."

"I'm in church, Carlos, so you know I'm telling the truth."

"Plenty lies are told in church, NikkiMac."

"Not by me, Carlos. I have my faults, but I work hard on telling the truth, even when it might not be comfortable to tell it." What I don't say is that I may not disclose everything. I give Carlos such a direct stare that he blinks hard twice before he returns to the topic of Sister Dallas.

"Sister Dallas must eat a lot of something, though. Maybe she loads up on sweets, breads, pasta, and ice cream. I never heard tell of a person porking up from vegetables. She looks like she weighs at least two hundred fifty pounds."

"It's not polite to talk about a woman's age or her weight, Carlos," Jacee bristles. "NikkiMac, I'm going to the dining hall. See you later, Brother Carlos."

"Goodbye, Sister Jacee. I'll see you two ladies at evening service."

Jacee and I find seats in the dining hall. The Kitchen Committee is in full effect today. Sister Carolina is sweating and directing folks. The Maze twins are running around like chickens with their heads cut off. Other brothers and sisters on the Kitchen Committee are trying to stay out of Sister Carolina's way.

She makes a loud announcement. "We would appreciate it if everyone would please take a seat at the eating tables. Our servers will bring the plates to you. Do you all hear me? Please take a seat. Stop coming up to the serving counter. We are making the plates at the counter, so please don't line up there. You may go to the dessert table and select a dessert after you have been served your dinner plate. Thank you!" Sister Carolina barks out commands like a drill sergeant, but a few bold souls still ignore her.

The dining hall is crowded because on dinner Sundays, people come who don't regularly attend worship. Not only do these delinquent adult members show up, they bring their children with them. Free food always draws a crowd. I think some of the neighborhood people also stop in for a free Sunday meal, minus a sermon.

"You know what I don't understand, NikkiMac? Why aren't these folks who haven't been at church since the last fellowship dinner embarrassed to come here today? It's obvious they only came because of the food!"

"Jacee, some folks have no shame. A couple of them came up to me today, shook my hand, and remarked how it's been a while since they've been here. Look at the brother right there; he's walking out with three plates wrapped in aluminum foil. I don't think he was even in worship service this morning. He just came to eat." We shake our heads from side to side. A server hands one chunky brother a plate. He looks at the food and promptly turns up his nose.

"Is there a problem, sir?" The sever looks concerned.

"I don't like dark meat chicken; I only eat the breast part of the chicken, the white meat. I don't know how many times I have to tell you people!" His attitude is haughty.

"Excuse me, brother. I didn't know that, but dark meat is all we have left." The young sister is trying to stay positive and composed.

"Well, I just won't eat any meat today. Bring me some bread and side dishes so I can fill up on them."

"I'll be right back, brother." She turns away, rolls her eyes skyward, and whispers, "Please, Jesus, help me deal with unlovely people."

"He must think he's at that fast food restaurant where he can have it his way," Jacee huffs.

"Jacee, at the restaurant, he'd have to pay for food and service. This is free, and that young sister is volunteering. She is not getting paid to deal with his funky attitude."

I catch the server's attention and give her a supportive nod and a smile. She smiles back and whispers, "Thanks."

Over at the serving area, Sisters Carolina and Honey shoo Brother Elton from behind the counter. "Why do you always hide Sister Melody's homemade German Chocolate cake? I know it's back there because Sister Melody asked me to carry it in for her this morning. I don't see it with the other cake slices on the dessert table, so somebody must be trying to take the whole cake home. I know that's what some of you committee people like to do. That's a crying shame." He moves away from the counter, but he's not happy about it.

"You don't know what you're talking about, Brother Elton," says Sister Honey, nervously patting her weave like she does when its glue makes her scalp itch. "We put all the homemade cakes out on the dessert table. The one you're looking for must have been eaten already."

"All I know is the good Lord sees everything, and He sees where you all are hiding that German Chocolate cake." Brother Elton notices Poppa Pace walk into the room and calls to him, "Brother Pace, what do you think about cake hoarding?" Brother Pace walks over, puts his arm around the shoulders of Brother Elton, and speaks softly to him. The body language of Brother Elton changes from cantankerous, to humorous, to calm. He walks to the dessert table with my Poppa Pace. Peace is restored.

Later, I ask Poppa Pace about the cake incident. "Daughter NikkiMac, I don't know why, but food often brings out the worst in some people. It makes no sense, because nobody here looks like they are starving, that's for sure. I simply asked Brother Elton to consider that he was in the

Lord's house, and after that wonderful sermon, he was about to have an argument about a piece of cake. That struck him as funny, so he smiled and calmed down. It often helps if you can get a person to see what they look like when they're ready to fight. He may be right; maybe someone on the committee does hide the donated food. I'll certainly mention that practice to our minister so he can address it."

"Poppa Pace, you're a wise man. Do you ever lose your cool?"

"I come close to it occasionally, Daughter NikkiMac, but I try to yield to the Holy Spirit to keep from acting like the devil."

Chapter 14   Little Sasha

Brother and Sister Coles are late, as usual. They enter the auditorium right after communion. With them is their daughter Sasha, who is two years old. Actually, the toddler is more in charge than either of her parents. Their comedic routine begins soon after they are seated. Mom sits Sasha on the seat between her and Brother Coles. Sasha says, "No," and crawls onto Sister Coles' lap. Mom places Sasha back on the pew. Another "No," from Sasha precedes the child climbing back onto Mom's lap. This goes on about five times before Sasha escalates and starts bawling. Sasha is quite a sight, with her twenty-plus tiny pigtails all over her head. Each pigtail is bound both at the scalp and the end with an elastic band that has marble sized plastic balls on it. I see red, blue, yellow, white, green, and orange ponytail holder balls. Sasha's headshaking makes them clack and clatter against each other. The colors and movement resemble a kaleidoscope. She has more ponytail holders than she has hair. Her chubby cheeks have a faint rose blush. She looks like a peach with eyes, nose, and a mouth.

The bawling has the desired effect. Sister Coles allows Sasha to sit in her lap. She gives Sasha a baby bottle. For now, the little one gets her way and she is happy. This doesn't last long, however, because after a few pulls on its nipple, Sasha wants to twirl her plastic baby bottle in the air. Her stubby fingers wrap around the bottle's tan nipple as she shakes her hand back and forth. Worshippers seated next to the Coles family slide over a little to get away from them. All except for Sister Preston, who is trying to ignore the commotion. Sasha swings more wildly with her bottle.

"Bop! Bop!" Sister Preston gets bottle-bopped on the side of her forehead. Sasha laughs, but neither Sister Coles nor Sister Preston do. Brother Coles wrestles the bottle from the child's grip.

Sasha screams, "No! No! No!" The battle is on.

Sasha wriggles and squirms while Brother Coles tries to hold her. Her fat hands slap her dad on the top of his head. It's like she's playing the bongos. He grabs her by her midsection, and holds his arms out to keep her hands from further battering his head. Her short legs flail at the air. They are dangerously close to the people sitting in the pew ahead.

"They can't do a thing with that child because they have spoiled her rotten," I whisper to Jacee.

"I know, don't you just want to snatch her?"

"Jacee, I want to snatch her and tap those legs. Then, I want to smack her parents for allowing her to get this way."

Sasha manages to get away from Brother Coles. She drops to the floor and disappears under the pew in front of her. The next time I see her, she's six pews forward, and she's pulling on the back of Sister Honey's hair weave. She turns around and waves with her other hand. Her eyes are so crinkled in glee that she doesn't notice her mom move in her direction. Sister Honey disengages Sasha's hand from her weave and holds onto the child's wrist until Sister Coles grabs it. Sasha is captured.

In the pulpit, Brother Johnson pauses from his point. "Little Sasha, are you trying to steal my thunder?" Laughter fills the room.

"By the way, the Education Committee has a Parenting Seminar scheduled here at the end of the month. Kindly read your church bulletins for the date and time. If you are a parent who can use this valuable information, please attend. If you are a parent who can help other parents, please attend. We are a Christian family, and in a family, members reach out to assist one another. The Bible gives sound advice about parenting. Write these scriptures in your notes and review them when you do your home Bible study: Ephesians chapter 6, verses 1 through 4. That's just one passage; I'll give you others during a coming sermon. Remember Christians, whatever wisdom we need in the way of living faithfully and abundantly, God has provided it in His word. Now, let's get back to my pre-Sasha sermon." Minister Johnson smiles warmly at Sasha and then he resumes preaching.

"Brothers, sisters, and visiting friends, I want you to look at Psalm 56. We must learn to constantly take our concerns to God in prayer. Look at David's plight in this Psalm. He'd been caught by the Philistines in Gath. That was tough for him. What did he do? He went to God for solution and solace. This is gut-level prayer, not all lofty and pretentious, trying to impress. David listed his concerns. He told the Father just what harmful things the people were doing to him. He asked God to deal with these oppressive people. We, as children of the kingdom, have to be just as intimate with God in terms of expressing what's troubling us. Our Father knows everything about us, but our faith in Him is shown when we turn to Him and simply ask for divine help. In prayer, talk to God plainly about your problems. Let Him hear that you *know* you need Him. Our comfort and confidence are expressed in verse 11 of this Psalm: pray to Him, trust Him, and don't be afraid. Live righteously before Him and your prayers will be answered according to His will."

My mind drifts to my struggle with the need for appropriate male companionship. Dates have been infrequent because most men back off when they realize we are not going to have a sexual relationship. The Bible teaches that sexual relationships are for married couples. Before I became a Christian, I didn't really think about that too much. Back then, I operated sexually based on how I felt. Sometimes I think I'd like to be married, but it's nothing to take lightly. Anyway, I haven't met that many available Christian men. Sometimes Jacee and I attend the National Conferences for Christian Singles, but the women there greatly outnumber the men. Too many of the brothers work that numbers game; they do some serious preening. These guys think they're a hot commodity and too many I've met are quite cocky. Even some of the less attractive ones turn up their noses at a sister who doesn't resemble a magazine cover model. I don't need that attitude. I can get that at the club, and my clubbing days are long over, thank God. Sometimes, a couple of the other single Christians here talk with me and Jacee about starting a singles group, but so far, no one wants to take the initiative. I'll probably end up organizing it. In the meantime, I am going to take my personal need for appropriate male companionship to the Lord in prayer.

Jacee taps me on my shoulder. While I was zoning out, Brother Johnson must have asked us to stand for the invitation song. "Wake up, NikkiMac. It's time to sing." I smile, stand, and join in *Leave It There*. At the end of the last verse, elderly but feisty Sister Blake begins her walk to the restroom. She holds on to her walker and slowly makes her way to the center aisle.

"I'm going to the bathroom," she whispers to anyone who gives her eye contact. "I can't hold it no more." Those who know the drill move their feet out of the way, because Sister Blake will run them over with the front wheels of her walker. She only got me one time, but when she did, she banged into the new corn on my left baby toe. I almost hollered out loud. I was two seconds away from knocking that old lady over before I caught myself. I'm so glad I did, because I love and respect old ladies. It was just a reflex reaction to the pain. I sucked it up and rocked back and forth. She kept on shuffling and pushing her walker. I don't think she even noticed me or my baby toe.

Chapter 15   TENT GOSPEL REVIVAL MEETING

"It's hotter than a firecracker out here! I'm about to burn up!" Jacee is spazzing.

"Hell is hotter, my sister," I tease.

"Girl, hush, the brother is calling worship service to order."

Jacee is right, though. It's a hot, humid Sunday morning and we are having an old-fashioned Church Tent Revival. Today marks the start. It will continue for the next five nights, from seven to nine o'clock. During tent revivals, we meet outside under this large blue tent in the church parking lot. There are folding chairs to sit on, not the cushioned pews. We have real warm air, not air conditioning. There are no walls or doors, and the tent side flaps are pulled back. We can see, hear, and smell the various sights and sounds of our urban community. Our guest minister, Brother Dawson Daniels, is from a sister congregation in Philadelphia, Pennsylvania.

"Good Sunday morning to you all. I am so blessed to be with you all today and for the rest of this week. I bring greetings from the church in Philadelphia. Let me start by praising Brother Obadiah Johnson's wife, Sister Sharlette Johnson. Before you get the wrong idea, I want to praise and thank her for that fine meal she prepared for me and her husband at their home last night. She put her foot in it, my friends! You all understand that saying, don't you? For those who are not familiar with that phrase, her food was extra delicious! I have not had chicken so perfectly fried, collard greens so tender, cornbread so sweet, potato salad so creamy, black-eyed peas so sassy, and sweet potato pie so luscious, in a mighty long while. I must also rave about the yellow cake with deep, dark chocolate icing." He pauses and pats his considerable belly. "I'd better watch out, or I won't be able to fit into my preaching suits that I brought with me!" We laugh warmly. Sister Johnson beams proudly, but nearby, Sister Melody and Sister Carolina look like a challenge has been thrown down. It would not surprise me if they prepared a meal or two for Brother Daniels this week; they both love their reputations for being great cooks.

"I know this worship setup is unusual for some of you, but those of us who've been around awhile know about tent revivals. Some twenty-five to thirty years ago, outdoor gospel meetings were popular. Church leaders used them as an evangelism tool. They felt that having a gospel meeting outside brought the gospel more to the people. Those who walked by would often stop, stay, and hear the gospel message. They felt more comfortable doing that than walking through the doors of the church building. Also, many congregations back then didn't have buildings large enough to accommodate the extra people who would come to revival meetings, so the big tents were more accommodating. Sometimes it is good to go back to the old ways. The purpose of a revival is to encourage and strengthen the members of the body and to evangelize those who are not in the body of Christ. We want to have souls saved, strengthened, and restored. Each of you, please make a commitment to come each night, and bring your neighbors, your coworkers, your friends and relatives. Join us these evenings from seven to nine o'clock. We will give a Bible answer for any Bible question relative to one's salvation. We plan to have a great time in the Lord."

This is my first tent meeting. I kind of enjoy the different surroundings but it certainly isn't as comfortable as inside; and for me, the distractions are significant. It doesn't take me long to notice a roly-poly robin feeding in the grass. Most of the women over forty fan furiously; the grand church hats slowly wilt. The pressed hair "kitchens" start to bead up as sweat wins over the effect of the hot comb. Attracted by the brightly colored outfits and aroma of perfume, a few bad-tempered yellow jacket wasps fly in and out of the tent. Hand fans are used to shoo them. One of the prayers is drowned out by the plaintive siren of a passing ambulance. Workers at the corner store across the street fire up the outdoor barbecue pit and contribute the scent of roasting pork. The bar on the other corner is open for business; the early bird customers sashay in for their afternoon drinks.

"Focus, NikkiMac, this is still worship." I scold myself and tune in to Brother Daniels.

"Please turn to the Old Testament book of Micah. Find chapter 6, verses 1 through 8. Here, God argues His case against His disobedient people. In verse 8, God tells them what He wants from them. Our Heavenly Father wants the same from us. He wants us to do what is right, love mercy, and walk humbly with Him. We can't live this way when we act indifferently towards Him. God knows when your heart grows cold to Him. He knows when and why you leave Him. Do you know when you are drifting? Let me give you some indicators. When you think God is your Big Daddy who lives in heaven and will give you anything you want, however you want it, you are drifting away. When you let Satan convince you that he is your friend, you are drifting away. Know that God's hand protects you from Satan, even when you're not aware of this protection. When you think formal worship is a replacement for a daily, conscious walk with God, you are drifting away. God needs your heart, all the time. Our worship is to stimulate our daily walk and our daily walk is to stimulate our worship. When you forget that your loving heart and kind acts glorify God, you are drifting away. Our Father wants us to deal with each other lovingly. Stop, look around this tent, and think. Do you see even a single person in this tent that you don't have a loving attitude towards?"

Minister Daniels pauses. People look around. Some shake hands in fellowship. I catch Brother Pace's attention and smile. He winks at me, and then turns to shake the hand of a brother behind him. Jacee and I hug each other the way best friends do. Then a chair scrapes the asphalt behind me, and I feel a tap on my shoulder.

"Hey, NikkiMac, do you love me too?" I turn around and look into the crazy face of Tasha Pace. Her loony eyes are eerily bright; her red lipstick is on her lips and on a couple of her front teeth also. She looks like a woman who's never found a mirror. I catch myself before I recoil from her tart breath and bizarre appearance.

"Tasha, I know you are as usual trying to get on my last nerve, but it is not happening today. I am glad to see you at church service, but you and I both know what I think about you. However, I am praying that the Holy Spirit will give me the power to love you in a Christian way. I even pray that you will return to the church."

"Look, Sister Pious, I am not trying to hear all that. I just want my dad to see me here, so he'll think I'm improving. I knew to sit near you because he's bound to look over here since you're his little pet. Just remember, he's my real father, not yours." Some of her stale spit flecks land on my cheek.

"Say it, don't spray it, you skank!" I sense that I am quickly losing my heavenly crown, so I bow my head and say a silent prayer of repentance.

"Tasha, your dad is waving at you. Why don't you go sit over there next to him?" On the surface, Jacee makes it sound like a request, but Tasha hears it as the command it really is. She moves to a seat farther away.

"Thanks, Jacee. I have got to do better about my feelings for her, because right now, she makes my butt itch."

"NikkiMac, you can't let your hatred for a nut like Tasha send you to hell. It is just not worth it." I know Jacee's correct. I'm about to say that to her, but a man brushes by us. He's being followed by Usher Gray.

"Excuse me, sir!" Usher Gray tries to get the attention of this person, who's leaving the tent meeting early, carrying a visitors' Bible. The small man, one of the neighborhood regulars, looks surprised that he's being followed. They meet outside the tent, near our seats. Usher Gray addresses the man again.

"Could I have the Bible back, please?"

"Oh, I'm sorry. I thought I'd keep it." The man appears nervous. He puts the Bible behind his back. Usher Gray notices this and reaches for the book. It slips out of the visitor's hand and falls to the sidewalk. Several bills spill out from the Bible's pages. At the same time, a woman rushes out to face the two men.

"Someone took money from my purse! They broke the snap on it! I brought twenty of my dollar bills with me, and now I only have ten of them!" She waves her hands and her broken, money-challenged purse wildly in the air. The usher and the apparent thief lock eyes for a second, before the small man takes off running across the street and into the nearest alley. Usher Gray helps the sister pick up her ten singles and retrieves the Bible. He even reaches in his pocket and gives her a ten dollar bill, which she gratefully accepts. Throughout this drama, service continues on.

Jacee passes a note to me. "Now you know that's a shame! Stealing and putting the loot in a Bible! Is nothing sacred?" I read the note and try to suppress a giggle.

I write a reply: "Ah, the joys of having church service outside in a lively urban setting!"

Chapter 16　Cletus in Church

I always enjoy hearing the warm greetings and laughter of my church family that takes place before the beginning and end of services. We, for the most part, genuinely take pleasure in each others' company. Jacee and I move around the auditorium and try to speak to as many people as possible before the bell rings. When it rings, people scurry to their seats. No one likes to be the loudmouth caught up in a lively conversation, oblivious to the fact that all are waiting for order so service can start. It happened to me once, and the person I was talking with did not even give me a hint as I yack-yacked loudly. Something finally told me to stop talking, maybe the fact that I noticed silence around me. It was so embarrassing. Since then, I try to get seated and become quiet at least a minute before service starts.

"NikkiMac, I'm finally here." I look to my left and see the shiny face of Cletus. He is definitely in church, and he's wearing the outfit that Poppa Pace helped him pick out a while ago. His chocolate face wears a beaming smile; his hair is short and neat. It looks freshly brushed. Normally, his teeth are tobacco-stained, but on this Sunday morning, they are a lighter yellow instead of brownish in color. He must have brushed them all night long.

"It's about time you got here, Cletus. You promised you'd come when you had a suit, and Brother Pace handled that for you a long time ago. Oh, let me stop fussing, because I am glad to see you. Give me a hug." Cletus and I hug, kind of. He's awkward, like he's not used to being warmly embraced in an innocent, affectionate, joyful manner. I notice his eyes aren't runny; they are almost clear and normal-looking.

"I haven't been around for a while, NikkiMac. A while ago, I got picked up by the po-po and the judge sent me to a different, longer rehab program. I'm trying to get it together. My mom is getting weaker. I need to help her out more. The program stressed that we need to change the people we hang out with and find a spiritual base, so I'm gonna try here for a bit. Plus, I did make that promise to you. It sure feels funny to be on the inside of the church building, though. I guess folks are wondering if I'm gonna ask them for some money."

"Don't worry about that, Cletus. God knows why you're here, and that's all that matters. Thank you for coming."

As soon as he sees Cletus, Poppa Pace comes over. "Well now, look who's here! I am happy to see you, young man." While they warmly grab hands and throw one arm over each other's shoulder in the man-handshake style, I turn to remark to Jacee about Cletus' improved appearance and direction. She's way across the room; I guess she took off while I was speaking with Cletus. I make a mental note to check her on her negative attitude. Cletus, unlike Tasha, seems to be trying to improve. Poppa Pace escorts Cletus around and introduces him to some of the brothers. I hear some people offer praise that Cletus is inside the building for worship instead of outside, hustling us for chump change.

A brother rings the bell to signal the start of service, and Cletus heads in my direction. I assume this is where he feels the most comfortable, so I move over to make room for him. Jacee elbows me, "NikkiMac, did you tell him he could sit with us? I do not want to be bothered with that crazy, bummy Cletus."

"Jacee, you need to stop. He's not crazy or bummy today. Instead, he's dressed appropriately and is in the Lord's house to hear the gospel. Your attitude is so wrong. Now, don't say anything else because he might hear you, with your non-whispering self." It's too late. The smile Cletus had when he left from where Poppa Pace sits is now gone. He actually looks a little hurt as he addresses Jacee.

"I heard what you said, Jacee. I don't know what your problem is with me, but at least I'm trying to do better. Why not give me a chance?" There is a pleading look in his eyes, but dignity in his posture. This is a different man from the one who used to be outside the church building asking for money.

At first, Jacee's large, hazel brown eyes stare him down, but she takes a second thought, hands him a visitor's Bible and mumbles, "I apologize, Cletus." I breathe a sigh of relief before we bow our heads for the opening prayer.

Afterwards, we sit and Brother Flowers goes to the pulpit, "Are there any prayer requests this morning?" He pauses.

"Yes, Brother Flowers, I have a request; it's actually more of an announcement."

"Well Sister Batts, since it's an announcement, you can give a note to one of the ushers and Brother Martin will read it during the announcement time."

"But since I'm already standing, I might as well speak my piece, Brother Flowers. That's my right as a child of God. Isn't that so, my fellow church members?" She looks around at the audience. We're silent, because we are not about to second any of her nutty showboating motions. The only sound we hear is an irritated "Stop!" from baby Sasha, who is attempting to wiggle out of mother's arms. Even though she sees she has no support, Sister Batts presses on. That's her way.

"Last Sunday night, someone hit my car in the church parking lot. I'm sure it was an accident. The person was probably trying to get out of a parking space, but my rear bumper sustained some damage. We all know that true Christians are honest and they accept responsibility for their actions. If you know you hit my car and won't tell the truth about it, you are a liar and the Bible says liars will be thrown into the lake of fire. I'd appreciate it if the person who did this would approach me today, so we can work this out. Also, if anyone saw what happened, please let me know today. That would be doing what is good, and the Bible says those who know to do good but don't do it are condemned. Thank you." Sister Batts casts a defiant look around the room, and then dramatically takes her seat.

"Some people just have to be seen," I whisper to Jacee.

"Somebody probably hit her car on purpose because she's always running her mouth and trying to have her way. She didn't have to barrel her way past Brother Flowers like that."

"Let us continue, brothers and sisters, with prayer requests." Brother Flowers emphasizes the last two words. I hope Sister Batts gets the message, because Brother Flowers looks like he means business.

Sister Longstreet stands and speaks. "Many of you know I have had trouble with my former boyfriend, Butch Mathers. Please pray that I keep faithful to the Lord and resist evil temptation. I also ask prayer for Butch, that he will come to the Lord. Not to be with me, but because it's the right thing for him to do. Please pray that all of us single Christians will live faithfully and be blessed with suitable mates, if it's the Lord's will."

A muscular man stands up to speak. His skin is the color of fried chicken; he looks to be almost a six-footer in height. He is handsome, not in a pretty boy way, but in a rugged way. He is boldly bald, and it truly works for his perfectly shaped head.

"Looky here, looky here," Jacee comments. Cletus hears her and looks uncomfortable. He probably didn't think he'd hear that type of admiration inside a church building.

"Some of you may not know me. I am Brother Lawrence Luke." His voice sounds like low rolling thunder coming from a distance. "I was baptized into the church some time ago, but I have not been attending services like I should. I make no excuses. I repent of this sin. I've asked God to forgive me, and I ask that you forgive me for forsaking the assembly. From now on, you will be seeing me at services regularly and we will get to know each other as Christians should."

"Amen, brother!"

"Welcome home!"

Brother Flowers offers prayer in response to the requests, and then we have the morning scripture reading. I reach over to help Cletus find the book, chapter, and verses in the Bible. He seems to appreciate this gesture; he's very attentive to the Bible reading.

Brother Vonner steps up to lead us in song. "Please turn your hymnbooks to *Worthy Art Thou*. Join me in singing praises to God." We sing, and I so enjoy the sound of our voices singing, with no instruments except the ones God built into our bodies. Our vocal chords, the breath He gives us, the lungs with their air capacity, our nasal and sinus cavities, our ears and our mouths-all are part of our marvelous human vocal instrument. It's a wonderful thing. Next, Brother Vonner leads *Blessed Assurance* and *We're Marching to Zion*.

"NikkiMac, some brother is pumping that bass line real tough!" Jacee is correct; it sounds like a new voice.

"I'm checking it out, Jacee. He is truly singing with conviction." The voice is coming from across the aisle from us. I sneak a peek; it's Brother Lawrence Luke, the one who asked for prayer earlier. He's into the song, too. Jacee and I raise our eyebrows, smile at each other, and keep singing.

Brother Vonner leads *I Gave My Life For Thee* before communion. The brothers selected to wait on the Lord's Table file in and conduct this part of the service. When they come near to us to pass the tray with the unleavened crackers, Cletus looks at me. I guess he wants to know if he should take communion, so I help him out. Now that he's finally here, the last thing I want is for him to feel uncomfortable.

"No, Cletus, you don't have to take communion. It's for those who are in the body of Christ. It's the way we remember and honor Him for dying on the cross for our sins and providing us with salvation."

"Oh," says Cletus, and he passes the tray to the next person. He does the same with the second tray that holds the small cups of grape juice. I am impressed with how closely Cletus follows the service. We sing *Hilltops of Glory* as Brother Johnson walks to the pulpit.

"Good morning, brothers, sisters, and visiting friends. Our main sermon text today is from Hebrews chapter 10, verses 19 through 25. Some assert that Hebrews was written by the Apostle Paul, others disagree. My purpose today is to focus on the message, for it applies to us today. The book of Hebrews was written to early Christians who were struggling in their new faith because they were trying to go back to their former faith. Some of them were even attempting to carry elements of their former faith into the gospel of Christ. The encouragement was for them to understand the superiority of Christ's sacrifice. The writer of Hebrews urged the Christians to persevere in the gospel and fully embrace Christian living. This Hebrew letter encouraged them to stay with Jesus, even though they faced challenges and persecutions from those who opposed the gospel. Look at verse 22 of this passage. Consider the privilege of drawing near to God! Christians, rejoice in your ability to come close to God through Christ! Hallelujah! This is an exclusive right to faithful Christians because of Christ Jesus' sacrifice for our sins."

"Amen! Amen!"

"Thank you, Lord!"

Brother Johnson continues to encourage us about the Christian joy of drawing near to God, holding on to the faith, and encouraging one another. Cletus asks me for a piece of paper and a pen so he can write down the scriptures and other notes. A glance at what he writes shows he is definitely literate. Everything is spelled correctly, and it's legible. Cletus has more going on in his head than I thought. People are not always what you think they are. I glance at Cletus; I'm so glad he came inside the church building today. Brother Vonner signals, "Song of invitation is *Victory In Jesus.* Let us stand and sing."

We stand for the invitation song. A man stumbles into the auditorium. He's obviously been drinking. He bobs and weaves down the center aisle. He heads for Brother Johnson's outstretched arms. On the way, he bumps into the end of a pew, holds on to keep from falling, and then bounces into the end of a pew on the opposite side of the aisle. He looks like the metal sphere in a pinball machine, bouncing jerkily from one side to the other.

"Thank you, Jesus and praise the Lord!" he shouts, and then falls into Brother Johnson. It's a good thing our minister isn't a tiny man, or they both might have gone down.

"Whoa, my friend! Are you alright?" Brother Johnson holds the man up and somewhat still by both arms, because his bouncy trip down the aisle made his legs wobbly.

"You the preacher?"

"Yes, I am. What can I do for you today?"

"I want me some Jesus. What I got to do to get me some Jesus?" Cletus hears the man's voice, and stiffens. I notice Usher Gray and Brother Sampson walking cautiously down the side aisles toward Brother Johnson and the rowdy, shaky visitor.

"Friend, do you mean that you want to be baptized into the body of Christ?"

"You mean get wet, in water?" The man looks incredulous. "Naw, I ain't tryin' to get all wet up. Can't you just pray over me an' throw a little water in my face?" He lets out a belch so loud that it wakes up a baby in the back pew. I know Brother Johnson's face is burning, because I smelled the alcohol fumes when the man stumbled past me.

"Friend, it seems to me you have been drinking alcohol, and quite a bit, judging from your lopsided walk down this aisle. I'm happy you feel the need for salvation, but you need to be sober so you'll know what you're doing when you confess Christ. You are welcome to stay for the remainder of the service and return any time you are ready. I will teach you what true baptism is, and why you need to be baptized into the body of Christ. Meanwhile, would you like a cup of coffee from our church kitchen?"

"Okay, preacher." This seems to be an agreeable proposal to our visitor. Brother Johnson signals Usher Gray, who moves to escort our woozy guest back up the aisle and toward the kitchen area. He can watch the rest of the service on the monitor while he sips coffee instead of whiskey. The man smiles at the usher and moves with him. However, when they get to our pew, the visitor spies Cletus and bares a snaggle-toothed smile.

"Cletus! My old drinking buddy! How you been, man? Long time, no see! Check this out." He reaches into the pocket of his jacket and pulls out a pint of some brown whiskey. He waves it around and tries to whisper, "Meet me in the kitchen and we can both have a swig." It doesn't come out as a whisper; it's more like an announcement. Some people hear his invitation and gasp. Brother Gray moves the man up the aisle faster and out of the auditorium. I have the feeling that he lost that cup of coffee offer when he made his last remark. Cletus looks devastated.

Jacee has, "I told you so!" plastered all over her face. Whispers can be heard around the room. Somebody even giggles.

"Don't feel bad, Cletus," I whisper. Being a drunk is your old lifestyle; it's in the past." I grab his hand and hold it tightly. I'm not sure why I feel so protective of Cletus at this moment, but I know I have an answer for anyone who says anything hurtful to him.

Brother Johnson returns to the pulpit. "By the grace of God, we have all overcome some worldly behaviors. If this man wants to know about and obtain salvation, by God's grace, it will be done. Please don't look down on him or anyone else, because that doesn't show a Christ-like attitude. Remember what the Bible says in First Corinthians chapter 6, verses 9 through 11. Focus on verse 11. All of us have flaws. We don't shine as brightly as we *think* we do." He smiles and looks over the congregation.

Cletus bows his head in embarrassment. "NikkiMac, I don't blame these people if they don't want me in here. They've seen me outside, hustling and getting high. A while back, I would have been glad to see Boopy and his bottle of whiskey. Matter of fact, I would have been figuring out how I could drink more of Boopy's whiskey than he could drink."

"Cletus, the Lord knows your heart. Any Christian in here worth the

salt that goes in his or her bread is joyful that you have heard the gospel."
I give him a supportive pat on his arm.

Brother Johnson continues, "Before I leave this pulpit, I want to
publicly thank Mr. Cletus for worshipping with us this morning. He is
in the right place and in the right frame of mind. Mr. Cletus, I pray that
you will keep coming to worship service and soon accept the invitation
to be baptized into the body of Christ."

"Amen," the congregation responds.

When the brothers collect the offering, Cletus runs his hands down
in his pockets and pulls out nothing but lint. "NikkiMac, I want to put
something in the offering basket, but I'm broke. Can I borrow a dollar?
At least this time you can see what I do with the dollar you give me." A
sheepish grin spreads across his face. I smile and slip a dollar to him. He
creases out the four corners and waits eagerly for the usher to bring the
collection basket to our pew. When it arrives, Cletus proudly places the
dollar in the basket, and then winks at me.

"That felt good, NikkiMac."

"Think how good it's going to feel when you give God your own
money, Cletus." He chuckles softly as Brother Martin comes before the
church.

"Good afternoon! It's now time for the announcements. The first one
is from the ushers, who say we are having too many cases of songbook
abuse." Brother Martin holds up a pitiful looking songbook. "Look at
this songbook. The cover has been totally torn off. There are pages that
have been torn out. Other pages have crayon scribbles on them. I'm told
that some of you are letting the children play with them. Songbooks are
not toys. If you need something to amuse your children, bring it with
you from home. These books are for worship; they are also not cheap.
The same thing goes for the Bibles and hand fans. Please, respect the
materials of the church." A couple of parents quickly take hand fans from
their babies.

"Brother Pace asks that we refrain from eating in the auditorium, or
anywhere else but the kitchen. Every Sunday after morning service, he
has to vacuum the carpets to pick up cereal, cookie crumbs, potato chips,
and crackers. He's sweeping up candy and gum wrappers. Also, someone
is leaving empty plastic soda bottles under the pews. What in the world
are some of us coming here for? Do we think this is the movie theater?

Actually, you're not supposed to leave your garbage in the theater, either, but they don't mind you eating there. This is church, not the cinema."

"That's right, brother!"

"Amen, Brother Martin!"

"I have a note that somebody is taking toilet paper from the restroom cabinets. Please stop doing this; it's stealing. If you need toilet paper that badly, please see me after service. I will give you some or get you some assistance so you can buy your own toilet paper."

"Amen, brother!"

"This is the end of our morning announcements. Please stand for dismissal prayer." After service, I turn to Cletus to shake his hand; this is our church custom. I expect Jacee to do the same, but she is about three pews away, shaking hands with other members. I hope she's not purposely avoiding Cletus.

"I guess she doesn't feel like giving me a chance today, NikkiMac," Cletus looks a little wounded, but only briefly, because several members reach out to him and greet him warmly.

"So, your name is Cletus. It's good to meet you. I'm Brother Sanders. Are you coming back to evening service?" The brother sounds sincere. He gives Cletus a firm handshake.

"I'd like to, but I have to go to my AA meeting, and then see about my ailing mother. My neighbor is with her right now, but I plan to be here next Sunday."

"That's great, Cletus. I'll look forward to seeing you next week. No matter what happens, don't stop coming to church."

"Thank you, man. I appreciate that. I do plan to keep coming here, because what I was doing wasn't working for me. I was fighting God and losing. I had Satan on my side, and I was still losing!" The two men share a laugh. I see others waiting to encourage Cletus, so I look for Jacee. She's over near the side entrance, cheesing at Brother Luke. Actually, it appears to be a mutual cheese fest, because Brother Luke is showing as many teeth as is Jacee. I decide to give them some space because I'm not wearing shades and all their grinning is blinding me. For a second, I wonder if I'm jealous that Jacee is getting attention from a Christian man who may be eligible. I'll have to think about that, but not right now.

Chapter 17   Antron in Trouble

Worship service is over. People greet one another in the lobby. As I near one of the front doors, young Antron barrels through and almost knocks me over.

"Hey! Whoa! Why are you running back inside the building like this? You're sweating! Are you alright?"

"Sorry, Sister NikkiMac. Help me!" He grabs my shoulders. I look into this teenager's eyes and see both fear and anger.

"Antron, is someone chasing you? Who's after you?" The indignation I experience whenever someone bothers a child rises inside me. Maybe it's my response to some things in my past.

Antron is about to cry, but I sense he won't do so in front of a crowd. I lead him to an empty classroom.

"Come, sit down and talk with me, son. What's going on? Where's your mom? I didn't see her in church today." Now that we are alone, his tears begin to flow. He lets me hug him while he cries, but he makes no vocal sounds, just breathing noises. His thin little bird chest heaves. Snot escapes his nose; I hand him some tissues. Antron blows his nose and tries to compose himself.

"My mom had to work, so she dropped me off here this morning. I'm supposed to ride home on the church van. She's coming to evening worship service. These dudes were chasing me. After church let out, I walked to the store down the street like I usually do. I like to buy some candy and a soda. But today, these guys I used to sometimes hang out with were in the store. When I was hanging out with them, we were all cool. But lately I decided to give them up because they started doing stuff that's not right, like jackin' other kids for their money, cell phones, sneakers, and stuff like that. I watched them do it, but I didn't do those things with them. It made me feel bad, so I figured I'd pay attention

93

to what my mom says and the things I learn at church so I won't get in trouble. Try to make some church friends. Anyway, now these dudes think I'm a punk. When they saw me in the store, I tried to play it off, speak to them and go about my business. The three of them went outside the store while I was at the counter paying for my stuff. When I went outside, they cursed at me and called me out of my name. Sister NikkiMac, I'll fight one person if I have to, but I got sense enough to know that all three of them would jump me. So I took off running back to the church building and that's why I ran into you. I was trying to get away to a safe place."

"Antron, you did the right thing; you can't fight three people. Is this a gang situation?"

"No, it's not a gang, just some dudes hanging out."

"Well, we're going to do something about it. This is probably a job for a man. I know your father doesn't attend this congregation, but is he in your life? Can you talk to him about this situation? If you give me his phone number, I can call him right now."

"My dad isn't around here and I hate to worry my mom with this. She's got enough on her mind."

"Do you mind if I ask Brother Pace to help us out?"

"Naw, I don't mind. Brother Pace acts like he cares about us kids here,everybody, really."

"I have to tell your mom, Antron. You are facing some trouble, so she has to know. But you have people here that will help you and your mom deal with this. We will work it out. I appreciate you telling me what's going on. You don't have to deal with this alone."

"Thanks for looking out, Sister NikkiMac."

"You are so welcome, Antron. You stay here while I get Brother Pace. Don't you worry." I wink at Antron, who now appears to be hopeful, and look for around for my Poppa Pace. I find him helping Sister Blake board the church van, so I wait nearby for him.

"How are you, Sister Blake?"

"Tolerable well, fine, I thank you, Sister NikkiMac." She's almost in, just needs help with her right leg and that big orthopedic shoe on her right foot. The shoe looks like it's too heavy for her skinny leg. She says she wears it to balance her out, because one leg is shorter than the other.

"Whew! I'm in, thank the Lord. Thank you too, Brother Pace. You sure are good to this here little old lady."

"Glad to help, Sister Blake. Now, what can I do for you, Daughter NikkiMac?"

Sister Blake chuckles, "You sure love NikkiMac like she's your own daughter, Brother Pace. I notice how you watch out for her and how you two have grown close over the years."

"Yes, Sister Blake, I've unofficially adopted her. She's a fine young lady who continues to grow in Christ."

"Well, Brother Pace, it helps her to have your fatherly support. Now, you just need to get her married off to a good Christian man!"

"I'm working on it, Sister Blake. You pray about it, also."

"Thank you both for discussing me like I'm not here," I say, and laugh. I believe they have my best interests at heart, so I don't really mind. We wave goodbye to Sister Blake and the rest of the passengers as the church van pulls off. On our way to the classroom, I explain Antron's situation to Poppa Pace. As usual, he listens closely. He notices my passion as I recount the panic in Antron's face when the child ran into me in the church lobby.

"Daughter NikkiMac, I can see this has really upset you."

"I know, Poppa Pace. A couple of my past experiences have made me real sensitive to children being wronged." He looks at me, and seems to know I don't want to go any further on this topic. We continue walking in silence. When he enters the classroom, Poppa Pace looks at Antron, smiles, and sits next to the teenager.

"Tell me what happened, son." Antron recounts his chasing episode, while Brother Pace gazes into the boy's eyes and quietly listens. The teenager finishes.

"First things first, I need a phone number. Does your mom have a cell phone?"

"Not anymore. It got stolen while she was at her job. There's a phone at our house, though. You can leave her a message."

"Okay, Antron. I am going to have Sister NikkiMac call your house and leave a message for your mother. She's probably called home from her job by now and is wondering why you didn't pick up the phone. Sister NikkiMac will let your mom know that I'll bring you home. You have a key to your house, right?" Antron nods. He does.

"Next, I need you to tell me the names of these boys who chased you." Antron slowly names the three boys. Brother Pace rubs his chin. "Antron, these first two boys are brothers; I believe their last name is Winston. The third boy you named is their first cousin; he's a Winston too. I know both of their mothers well; they're sisters. They used to work with me at the post office. I bet they don't know what their boys are up to. We need to talk with these boys, your mom, and their mothers. I'd like to talk with their fathers, but neither of them is around. Antron, is your dad in Trenton?"

"No, Brother Pace. My dad is in jail. I haven't seen him since I was five years old. I have a couple of pictures of him, that's all." Antron looks embarrassed by his admission. "Brother Pace, these dudes already call me a punk because I don't hang with them anymore. I really don't want any trouble."

Brother Pace puts his hand on Antron's shoulder. "Son, you're already getting trouble from them, and it will probably get worse. If their mothers knew about these boys' behavior, they would have a fit. Their mothers work hard, and they want their boys to go straight, not straight to the juvenile justice system. I recognize that you don't want them to see you as a 'snitch', but sometimes you have to tell someone to make things better for everyone. Antron, I've got your back, but more importantly, God has your back. Maybe God put me and you together for this very reason."

"Antron, I know for a fact that Brother Pace can help you; he was there for me when I was in a dangerous situation." I hold the teenager's hand.

Brother Pace continues, "These boys are 'wannabe' thugs. They can't and don't want to handle being in an organized gang. They just want to mess with kids they think are weak. First, let me speak to these three boys and their mothers. Then I'll get you, your mom, and us all together. We'll work this out." I give both Antron and Poppa Pace a hug and leave the classroom. I know that the young man is in capable hands.

In the parking lot, I'm accosted by the raucous sounds of a male and female arguing. A couple is passing by on the sidewalk outside the church gates, hollering at each other. I recognize them, since they walk past often on Sundays, but I don't know their names. Sometimes they stop and look over at the church building, but they never enter the gates. Their dress, their walk, and their expressions look crazy. They have the look of people who used to get high off some substance, then stopped getting high, but didn't stop soon enough to regain normalcy. Some people call this the "fried brains" syndrome. The couple is wearing clothes with multiple prints and both have on leather boots, even in this hot weather. His hair is braided on one side but the other side is loose, sticking straight up. She has her head wrapped in many scarves with bright colors. She carries a purse in her left hand and a Bible in her right hand. Now that I think about it, every time I've seen her walk by, she's had a Bible in her right hand. I take out my remote so I can unlock the car and get in quickly if I must. Occasionally, folks like this can be erratic, friendly one minute and argumentative the next. Like I do with Mad Maggie, I give them their space and try not to get on what's left of their nerves.

The man hollers at the woman, "You poor thing. You just as crazy as you wanna be!"

The woman responds, "I know you are not calling nobody crazy, with your tired tail!"

"You didn't say that last night, now did you? Last night you was callin' out my name!"

"Man, don't be puttin' my business out in the street like that! You keep talkin' trash and I'm gonna knock you in your head so hard your eyes are gonna be lookin' for each other!" The woman scores on that line; it's funny to me, so I laugh, but that draws unwanted attention. The man focuses on me.

"Hey, church lady! You hear how my woman talks to me? Next time you go inside your church, ask the preacher to pray for me, because she is dangerous!" I try to be invisible and walk more quickly to my car. The last thing I feel like being caught up in is a crazy people drama.

"Shut up, you fool! That woman don't wanna hear your nonsense!" They stop walking and each one hangs on to a fencepost. Maybe they enjoy having an audience.

"Hey, church lady. Guess what my woman did to me in our kitchen this morning? She slapped me upside the head with a big ear of Jersey corn and then hit me in the back of my head with this here family Bible. I ask you, is that the Christian thing to do?" I reach my car, cracking up inside, but trying not to show my amusement.

"You two have a good afternoon. Please come to our worship service sometime soon." The woman stands up straight and finds a serious facial expression. She looks at me through narrowed eyes and responds.

"We may just do that, but when we show up at church, don't look at us like we a couple of turds."

"I promise not to do that, and neither should anyone else." The woman looks at me for a while and says nothing. Then she nods at me, grabs her partner, and they begin to move on. When I leave the church driveway, I wave as I drive past them. They wave back. He wraps his arm around her waist, and they go on their merry way, talking all the while. I can't help but grin when I think about that couple. They may be a little nutty, but at least they have each other.

I check the rearview mirror. Suddenly, I catch my breath. Right behind me is a black SUV with the name DARIUS on the vanity license plate. The vehicle looks newer than the one I remember, and it's a different style, but that license plate is a tell. I have not seen Darius Muse since he assaulted me at Club Taste all those years ago. I figured he had left town, although that's not necessary to not be seen in Trenton.

Our city has an interesting dynamic. Although it's the state capital, with a population of about 83,000 people, it's the kind of place where you can mind your own business and not be seen unless you put forth effort to do so. You might occasionally bump into someone from your high school days at the grocery store, at an event at the Arena in south Trenton or at the War Memorial Building, or at the annual Heritage Days Festival. However, you may never see that same person on a regular basis. If you don't run in the same circles with someone, like church, a beauty salon, a sorority/fraternity, or a bar, you might not see certain people for years at a time. Trenton is the kind of place where one has to make a conscious effort to interface with people outside of one's circle. That's interesting, too, because I think the land area of Trenton is only about 7.5 square miles. I don't know, maybe it's also like that in other cities this size.

The black vehicle is still behind me, but after a few blocks, it turns onto a side street. I breathe a sigh of relief. Maybe it's another Darius. Maybe it's not Darius Muse.

Chapter 18   Darius Found, Sister Flossie Lost

I was wrong; Darius Muse is definitely in Trenton. More specifically, he's here in church, wrecking for me what was an otherwise fine Sunday morning. Jacee notices my tension during the singing of *Where Could I Go*; she asks me if I feel ill. As I sing the words to the hymn, I wish I could go to the land of the invisible.

"Jacee, remember when I told you about my last night at Club Taste and the guy who hit me? The night Brother Pace came to my rescue?"

"You mean Darius Muse? Yes, I remember, but what has that got to do with anything? I thought he left town soon after that situation with you."

"I don't know whether he left town or not, but his black behind is sitting up there on the first pew!"

"NikkiMac, you can't be serious, what's he doing in church?" Before I can reply, Brother Pace steps to the pulpit, whispers something to Brother Vonner, and the song leader moves aside.

"Brothers and sisters, we have a bit of a situation here. Sister Flossie Johnson, our minister's elderly mother, seems to be missing from the building. Those of you who know her are aware that her mind doesn't work as well as it used to, and she tends to wander. I'm told she was escorted to the restroom, but it appears her escort did not walk Sister Flossie back into this room. We just want to be certain she hasn't wandered from the building out onto the streets. Has anyone seen Sister Flossie within the last ten minutes?" People whisper. No one raises a hand to report seeing Sister Flossie. The ushers search around the building and grounds. Minister Johnson and his wife Sharlette do the same. Sister Sharlette usually watches over Sister Flossie, but I did notice earlier that she was busy welcoming and introducing a female visitor to others. She must

99

have asked young Sister Blanche to take Sister Flossie to the restroom; because Blanche is spazzing and looking pitiful while she explains.

"I had to run back and get my purse because I made a mistake and left it on the church pew. My rent money is in it. I brought it to church with me because I can't leave money at my apartment when I'm not there. I can't trust my roommate's children. I was only gone from the restroom for a minute. I thought I'd be back before Sister Flossie was finished." People next to the young woman attempt to comfort her.

Brother Vonner speaks to the congregation. "We have the ushers and others looking all over the place. We will find Sister Flossie. Let's ask God for help." We bow our heads; some people hold hands.

"Our Father in heaven, holy is your name. You know all things, so you are aware we need you to put your arm of protection around our dear Sister Flossie. Give us wisdom and guidance in our efforts to locate her."

"Amen, Father."

"Help us, Father God."

"Dear Father in heaven, please comfort our Sister Blanche, who went with Sister Flossie to the restroom. Help her not feel devastated or be treated coldly because of her mistake. She did not mean for anything bad to happen. Bless us to get through this experience victoriously, Father. We ask in the name of Jesus. Amen."

The church says, "Amen." Brother Vonner begins to announce the next hymn, but we hear splashing sounds and laughter. It's coming from the baptistery located behind the pulpit. It sounds like the noises children make when they play in the bathtub.

Someone calls from the audience. "Open the baptistery curtains! It sounds like there's somebody back there in the water!" Brother Johnson and two ushers rush to the platform and yank the curtains open. There sits Sister Flossie, wet and happy as a pig in slop! She's sitting on one of the steps that lead down into the water. Her knee high stockings are off her legs and tied around one wrist. Her bare legs and feet splash in the water. The congregation laughs, cheers, and praises God.

"Momma, what are you doing in this water? Come on, let me help you!" Brother Johnson takes off his socks and shoes and enters the water. He gently coaxes his mother up the few steps.

"I'm fine, Sonny. I just felt like getting my feet wet, that's all. My legs came along for the ride." When she notices the congregation watching, she grins and waves.

"Momma, you had us all worried about you." Minister Johnson looks out at the audience. "Excuse me, brothers and sisters, we're going to close the curtains and get my mother out." Sister Sharlette, who looks greatly relieved, moves to assist her husband and her mother-in-law.

"Brother Flowers, could you please lead us in a prayer of thanksgiving? The Lord surely heard and answered our prayer to find our sister, my dear mother. After prayer, let's continue the service."

Brother Flowers walks to the front. "Let's all stand and bow our heads in reverence to God." The congregation gets ready for this prayer of thanks. "Dear Father, we know you do all things well. We thank you for hearing and responding to our prayer for our Sister Flossie. Please continue to be with us. I pray that our worship will be pleasing and acceptable in your sight. In Jesus' name we pray. Amen." Brother Flowers asks us to be seated. Then, Brother Vonner leads us in *Revive Us Again* and *God Will Take Care Of You*.

Jacee turns to me. "NikkiMac, how in the world did Sister Flossie get from the restroom to the baptistery, without anyone noticing her?"

"Jacee, the only way I can think of is through that wide door that leads from the street to the rear of the baptistery. Brother Pace once mentioned to me that the builders had to take the baptismal pool in through that particular door, because of the weight and size of the pool. He and the other maintenance staff members normally keep it locked from the outside, but someone must have goofed. Sister Flossie probably walked out of the restroom, through the crowd in the lobby, out the front doors, and around to that rear baptistery door. She may have thought she was reentering the auditorium through the regular back door."

"Well, NikkiMac, once she saw the water, she clearly made another plan! Can you believe she took off her knee highs and got to splish-splashing in the 'holy water' like that?" Jacee amuses herself.

"I know, she is a trip! Oh, it's time for communion." The five brothers selected to wait on the Lord's Table file in. There is prayer for the bread and the fruit of the vine. The five brothers take communion themselves and begin to pass the trays, starting at the front of the auditorium. I catch my breath when I see Darius Muse take and eat the communion cracker and drink the fruit of the vine. I don't think he's a member of the church, so he must simply be imitating the people around him. It's hard for me to accept that Darius Muse is here for any good reason; he's got to be up to something. Maybe he has his eye on one of the sisters. I hope not, because any man who physically abuses a woman is a dog, as far as I'm concerned. I take my mind off Darius, because he is not the reason I'm here today, and my focus should be on Jesus and His sacrifice for me. Following communion, we sing *Since Jesus Came Into My Heart*, and during the chorus of the fifth verse, Brother Johnson takes his place at the pulpit.

"Brothers and sisters, the sermon today is from the book of Mark. The chapter is 10; the verses are 17 through 22. Please follow along in your Bibles as I read aloud. In the Lord's church, we want you to see for yourself what the Bible says; and not just assume that any preacher who steps in front of you is telling you what the Bible says. Your soul is too valuable to leave to chance."

"That's right, brother." We read the passage from our Bibles together.

"In this passage, the Bible tells us about a conversation between a rich young man and Jesus. The man sought the counsel of Jesus to find out how to obtain eternal life. First of all, let's look at the contrasts. The man was rich in material things; Jesus had nothing in the way of material wealth. The young man had position; the Bible refers to him as one who had the rule over others. Jesus left the throne in glory to come to earth and have no position. The ruler did at least three things right. He came to the right person. He asked the right question. He obtained the right answer. His wrong move was refusing to act on the right answer, because verse 22 tells us he sadly walked *away* from Jesus. He just could not let go of his wealth, even to gain eternal life! He left the source of eternal life to hold onto earthly wealth, something which won't last forever. What's that old saying? The answer to my question is that you never see a moving van attached to a hearse. Think about it. You can't take your money with you when you leave this earth!"

"Amen, preacher!"

"Teach it, Brother Johnson!"

"But let us not be too hard on the young ruler, because many of us have something *we* need to give up for Jesus, so we can get closer to Him. If we don't need to give it up, we need to put God in front of it. Does a material possession have more of your attention and devotion than Jesus? Does your job have more of your focus than serving the Lord? Does a man or a woman have more of you than you give to God? Think about it, Christians and visiting friends. Have you counted the cost of losing your soul?"

"Preach, man!"

"Amen! Amen!"

Brother Johnson stops talking, descends from the pulpit, walks back and forth in front of the front pews, and down the center aisle. Then, he stops walking, and continues the sermon. "This message is for all of us, but I especially want to appeal to those who have not been baptized into Christ. Here's the way to enter the kingdom, in five easy steps. First, you must hear the gospel: how Jesus Christ died for the forgiveness of our sins. Check out Romans chapter 10, verse 17. You heard the gospel this morning. Second, believe what you have heard. See John chapter 8, verse 24. Third, repent of your past sins. See Acts chapter 17, verse 30. Now, let me park here for a minute. Remember the rich young ruler? He did not want to make a change in order to obtain salvation. A lot of us don't want to come to Christ because we don't want to turn away from some activity, friend, or thought pattern that is contrary to the will of God. Is anybody listening?"

"That's right, brother!"

"Yes, yes! Teach it!"

"Two more steps to go. Fourth, confess Jesus Christ as the Son of God. You can find this in Matthew chapter 10, verse 32. It's not a complicated action; all you do is publicly acknowledge that Jesus is God's Son. Fifth, be baptized into Christ, for the forgiveness of your sins. You can read about this in Acts chapter 2, verse 38. At your baptism, you are granted the Holy Spirit to assist you in living righteously before God. I ask you, what's keeping you from Jesus? Don't walk away sorrowfully like the young ruler did. Come to Jesus today." Brother Vonner starts off *Almost Persuaded* as we stand and join him. I close my eyes and let the words of the song rush over me, until I hear Jacee.

"Uh, uh, I do not believe what I am seeing!" It's Darius Muse, and he's walking to Brother Johnson! I quickly shut and open my eyes again, but I still see Darius, and he's still walking to Brother Johnson. People around me exclaim and praise the Lord for this, but I do not. I'm pissed off because I believe this is some kind of stunt he's pulling. They say a leopard doesn't change his spots, and Darius is a sure enough leopard. The invitation song ends and we sit down. Brother Johnson and Darius speak quietly to each other. Then, our minister and Darius face the congregation.

"Brothers and sisters, this is Darius Muse. He has been quietly attending our Thursday evening evangelism class for a few weeks. Darius has been listening and following along in his Bible as the other class members learn how to tell others about Christ. He's also met with me a few times to ask questions pertaining to his salvation. Darius now realizes that he is not a Christian. I invited him to come to worship, and he did so today. He wants to be baptized into Christ, but wants to say a few words to the congregation before I take his confession."

Darius takes the microphone offered to him by Brother Johnson. That's when I notice that only one of Darius' coat sleeves has a hand extending from it. He's missing his left arm, from the elbow down.

"Thank you. Minister Johnson is right. It wasn't until I started studying the Bible with him and some of the other brothers here that I realized I needed salvation. I didn't know I was a sinner in God's eyes. I knew I did a few wrong things, but generally, I thought I was a pretty good person. I know I am better than I used to be, because I did some bad things in my past and one of them I want to address now." I feel a weird sensation in my gut, and grab Jacee's hand.

Darius clears his throat and continues. "Many years ago, I was disrespectful to one of the sisters in this church. I don't think she was a member then, because we were both in a place where one doesn't usually see Christian folk. Anyway, she wasn't doing anything to deserve this treatment by me, but I tried to come on to her with force. When she refused my advances, I slapped NikkiMac in the face."

It is so quiet that I can hear myself breathing. I want the floor to open up, swallow me, and save me from this embarrassment. My face gets hot. I feel like my freckles are running around on my face, colliding into one another in discomfort.

Darius looks at me. "NikkiMac, you are soon to be my sister in Christ. I am so sorry I hurt you that night. Will you please accept my apology and forgive me?" I shift from embarrassment to anger at what I see as grandstanding by Darius. All eyes are now on me.

"Darius, that happened many, many years ago. No, I was not a Christian then. But I am glad that night happened, because it caused me to meet Brother Pace, who rescued me from you, if you recall. I forgive you, Darius. Now I want you to honestly answer *my* question. Do you forgive me for biting you in retaliation for the slap you gave me that night?" Folks are probably getting whiplash from looking back and forth between Darius and me.

"I forgive you, NikkiMac." The congregation stops holding their collective breath and applauds. Brother Johnson then takes Darius' confession and service continues while brothers prepare for the baptism. During the collection of the offering, I feel Jacee watching me protectively.

"I'm okay, Jacee. Stop being a mother hen."

"He didn't have to say all that in front of everybody. That was most definitely TMI: too much information. All he had to do was repent of his past sins, including that behavior with you, and be baptized. Then, he could come to you privately and ask your forgiveness. I don't get why he had so much to say. He should have been saying what happened to his left arm. He sure had it years ago when I saw him last. If he has so much of a desire to tell something, let him tell that."

"Thank you for your support, my dear sister." I feel a little better. Soon, the curtains open. Darius steps down into the water and is baptized. Only God knows a person's heart; I hope Darius isn't playing with Him. After service, Poppa Pace rushes over while Jacee and I shake hands with others.

"Daughter NikkiMac, are you alright? I tried to get to you when Darius came in this morning, but I got caught up with the Sister Flossie situation. Minister Johnson mentioned to me that Darius was back in town and had started to attend the evangelism class, but I really didn't think much about it. I guess I've been a little preoccupied lately. Forgive me for not mentioning it sooner." I make a mental note of his remark about preoccupation; he's generally the most focused person I know. I hope everything is okay with him. Maybe that trifling Tasha is acting up more than usual.

"Thanks, Poppa Pace. I'm alright. I'm glad he's been added to the kingdom, but I still don't trust him. The Lord says we have to forgive others in order to be forgiven, and I do forgive Darius. But, I truly need the Holy Spirit to help me have a Christian attitude toward him. Who would've ever thought that Darius would be my brother in Christ?"

"I'll be leaning on the Holy Spirit for that attitude myself," snorts Jacee.

Brother Pace smiles and offers, "You both will be alright. I'll see you later; I've got to take care of some things in the building."

Something catches Jacee's attention. "Sister Batts is over by the gate talking with Brother Carlos; let's go rescue him, NikkiMac." We stroll to the gate. Sister Batts has her back to us, but mischievous Carlos sees us approaching.

"Brother Carlos, do you believe that about Sister NikkiMac and our new brother who was baptized today?" It sounds like Sister Batts is about to get her gossip on.

"Do I believe what, Sister Batts?"

"That she used to be a prostitute who solicted men in the bars. That she got money from Darius for sex, but then didn't give him sex. He was trying to get what he paid for and that's why he slapped her." She gets whisper- close to Carlos, but doesn't talk softly. She can't do that anyway because she has too much bass in her voice. Jacee and I can clearly hear her.

Carlos protests. "Sister Batts, how did you get that story from what Darius and NikkiMac said in church? I didn't hear what you just said come out of their mouths. Even if they had said that, who doesn't have something in their past life that they are ashamed of? I surely can't claim that, can you?"

Jacee and I walk to the front of Sister Batts. Before I can speak, Jacee spurts, "I do not believe you, sister. You just left church service; you are still on church property, and you are starting gossip. You are old enough to know better. Shame on you!"

I stare Sister Batts square in the face. "Perhaps you need to repent of your sins of the tongue, my sister. I can give you some scripture for that by book, chapter, and verse. But since you claim to be such a Bible scholar, I'm sure you know where to find it. Here's another FYI: I know you've been sniffing around Brother Pace. I don't think he'd appreciate a woman admirer who gossips, especially one that gossips about me." Sister Batts shakes her head; her long skinny legs shake a little. Then, she shifts her weight from one foot to the other. "I am going to pray for you,

Sister Batts, because your careless and inaccurate talking may negatively influence others. Is there any other information you wish to share about me at this time?"

"No, Sister NikkiMac. Umm, I've got to go now." With that, the self-proclaimed Bible scholar makes a beeline to her car. It's the first time I've ever seen her back down from a confrontation. Carlos and Jacee laugh out loud. It's contagious.

Carlos catches his breath. "See how rumors get started? NikkiMac, does she have an issue with you? Why would she flat out lie about you like that?"

Jacee quickly speaks up. "NikkiMac is right, Sister Batts does like Brother Pace, but other than being his usual polite self, he doesn't pay any special attention to her. I think she believes that NikkiMac is blocking her."

"Jacee and NikkiMac, has Sister Batts ever been married?"

"Her husband divorced her and left the church years ago. She announced it once in the Sisters' Bible Class when they were discussing who could and could not scripturally remarry. Her position is that since her husband divorced her, she can marry again as long as she marries an eligible Christian man." I remember being in that Sisters' Class and ending up somewhat confused by all the scenarios presented. Maybe I wasn't paying enough attention.

"She probably scares most men off with that attitude of hers," Carlos offers.

I shrug and dismiss this episode so I can mess with Carlos. "You'd better watch out, Carlos. After all, she did have you cornered out here. Maybe she's planning on getting with you, if things don't work out with Brother Pace."

Now it's time for me and Jacee to laugh, and we do. Brother Carlos doesn't.

Chapter 19   It Is What It Is

Ever since he rededicated himself to Christ, Brother Luke has attended church services on a regular basis. He continues to show interest in Jacee, and she appears to be enjoying this. I'm happy for her, but I am cautiously optimistic, because I know even some church men think it's okay, or at least excusable, to have sex without marriage. I've been given various reasons why:

"It's not possible to be celibate because it's unnatural. That's why God gave humans a sex drive."

"It's okay if two people are having sex exclusively with each other."

"Before committing to marriage, you have to find out if you are sexually compatible."

"God meant for us to love one another. Love includes sex."

I believe I've pretty much heard every rationale out there. Just last year, one brother, who was more interested in the size of my butt than the state of my soul, tried to hit on me. I can still see his nickel-slick player expression as he eased over to me that day.

"Sister NikkiMac, you seem like a fine Christian single woman. I can't believe you're not married. You certainly are quite attractive. I'm single too, and sometimes it gets real lonely. I don't date worldly women. I need a like-minded spiritual woman. Why don't we go out for a cup of coffee, or to dinner? We can get to know one another better."

"Well, brother, that would depend on what you mean by us getting to know one another better. I'm single and I practice celibacy." It's none of his business that during my years of being in the church I've had struggles with this. Those failings have made me more watchful. I don't like to waste time, so it's easier for me to find out right from Jump Street if sex is on a man's agenda.

"Sister NikkiMac, all I'm talking about is two single Christians developing and exploring a friendship. You know what some folks say about intimacy between two Christians: 'Two clean sheets can't dirty one another', or something like that. Anyway, some Christians have sex, but then they ask God for forgiveness."

I remember rolling my eyes up in my head before I rolled them back down and looked him squarely in his face. "So, basically, you support premeditated consensual sin, is that it? The Bible says there is no forgiveness for that. And another thing, call it what it is; it's fornication. I'm sure you know the Bible condemns it. Have you read chapter 6 of Romans?"

His feathers ruffled at my response; he backed off after a final word. "Oh, there you go, getting all preachy. Look, my sister, I didn't mean to offend you; I've just been checking you out, and thought we might be cool together."

"Thanks, but no thanks, brother." There were no hard feelings on my part then, and this brother still shakes my hand in greeting at church, but he hasn't said anything else to me about his philosophy. He is rumored to be a bit of a church "player", so I guess some women have accepted his definition of acceptable behavior for single Christians.

Brother Luke and Jacee enter the pew; they've been coming to church together lately. He sits next to her; she sits next to me. "Good morning, Jacee and Brother Luke, it's good to see you both this Sunday morning."

"Hey, NikkiMac, how are you doing today, my sister?" Jacee gives me a warm hug.

"Happy Sunday, Sister NikkiMac." Brother Luke gives me a firm handshake. I certainly prefer a firm handshake instead of the limp handshakes some people give. They barely grip your hand as they slide their palm and fingers against yours. It's creepy.

Brother Flowers rings the bell to indicate the start of service. He asks for prayer requests and gives the opening prayer. Those who are still standing and chatting quickly find their seats. Sister Coles rushes to scoop up little Sasha. This cuts short the child's flight to freedom. Other vigilant mothers perform their head rotations to see where their preteen and older children are seated. The unwritten rule for a child being allowed to sit away from the parent requires that said child sit where he or she can be seen by mom. That way, mom can give her child *The Look*, which is nonverbal communication that squashes inappropriate behavior. Old school moms have it in their behavior management arsenal. Teenager Antron Baker takes his place next to Poppa Pace, who appears to have worked out the situation between Antron and the Winston boys. Antron is happier and more secure, now that Poppa Pace has taken him under his wing. It looks like Brother Pace has another church child.

Brother Flowers looks over the crowd. "Are there any requests for prayer? If so, please stand and make your requests known." Sister Blake raises one hand, then grasps her walker and scoots forward in her seat so she can stand. "I see your hand, Sister Blake. Please don't get up. You may make your request from your seat."

"Thank you, Brother Flowers. I am asking for prayer for my overall health; but I also want to give praise to God. My old doctor said I might have to get my big toe cut off because of my bad sugar problem. I hurt that toe months ago and it wasn't healing right. Do you know what I did? I will tell you. I took my ailing toe to the Lord in prayer and asked Him for wisdom and healing. He heard me, because soon after that, a sister here told me about another doctor and I went to see him. He prescribed a different treatment, and my toe is healing! Praise God! You never know how God is going to bless you, but He makes a way." The congregation reacts strongly.

"Hallelujah!"

"Praise His holy name!"

"Thank you, Jesus!"

"Thank you for your request, testimony, and praise, Sister Blake. Does anyone else need special prayer?"

A brother whose name I don't know stands. "I ask the church to pray for me because I have sinned. I reacted to an aggressive driver by giving him the finger when he cut me off. I probably wouldn't be standing up to say this, but my car has a bumper sticker on it that advertises the church. I realize that my obscene gesture made the church look bad in the eyes of the world. Please forgive me, brothers and sisters." I hear a couple of giggles, and then Cletus stands.

"I'd like the church to pray for my mother. She's in her nineties, doesn't see too well, and has a hard time getting around. Please pray for her well being. I am thankful that the Lord helped me get clean and sober in enough time to be of assistance to her. I ask for God's grace to continue to be free of alcohol, at peace, and joyful in the Lord. Pray for both of us, please."

"God bless you, Brother Cletus."

"Hold to His unchanging hand, Brother Cletus."

I'm thankful for the encouragement most Christians here give to Cletus. They see he's trying hard to do what's right, for God, himself, and for his mother. My heart goes out to him; he's done a 180 degree turn since his alcohol abuse treatment and his baptism into Christ. God is making him into a new man. We bow our heads and Brother Flowers offers prayer.

After that, Brother Leethan comes before the group. "Please turn to *More About Jesus*, and sing with me, church." I am impressed with the humble spirit he displays as he leads us in song. It is clear that he enjoys singing for the Lord. Jacee taps me on my leg and nods her head toward the aisle. As usual, Sister Keke Lewis rushes past on her way to a pew near the front. She's constantly a little late and all the time heads for the front pews.

"She always looks like she comes here straight from the all night disco!" I smile and shake my head; Jacee has a point. Sister Keke sports really big hair, short and tight- looking stretchy dresses, glittery high-heeled shoes, big hoop earrings, and lots of makeup. In contrast to her appearance, she has a quiet and gentle demeanor. She's been a member for a few years, but I don't know much else about her.

"Sisters, she probably wants to looks her best, and those outfits may be her best ones. At least she comes to church." Brother Luke breaks a girlfriend rule by stepping into a conversation between two women. There is something about his tone that I don't like, and I file this information for future reference. Jacee doesn't seem fazed by his remarks; she resumes singing. I file that piece of information, too. Brother Leethan starts *Kneel At the Cross*, but by the third verse, I must excuse myself to go to the restroom. I push open the double doors leading to the lobby and in my urgency, I bump into Usher Gray.

"Oops! I'm sorry, Brother Gray." His eyes narrow at the sight of my moving feet; I'm breaking the "Stay in your seat" rule.

"Sister NikkiMac, you need to slow down and watch where you're going!" I need to pee too badly to waste time with him, so I keep my mouth shut and keep on moving. I make it to the stall just in time. Two women enter the restroom. I can't see anything but their shoes, but I can clearly hear the excitement in their voices.

"Girl, did you see Brother Adam Greene today? He is so fine!"

"That's the reason I come to this church, to get my eyes massaged by Brother Adam's fineness! I'm not a member here; I go a different kind of church, but my church is having a boring speaker this month. I figured I'd check out this cutie and shake his hand, at least."

"Did you see him last Sunday? Girl, when he stepped up there in that gray suit and striped tie…" I see her feet move like she's walking around in a circle.

"Thank you, Jesus! Hallelujah!"

"He does make me want to shout, but they don't do that in this church."

"Whatever! Do you know if he's dating any woman here?"

I flush the toilet, exit the stall, and move to the sink to wash my hands. In their Adam-lust, they hadn't earlier noticed my presence. Now, they look startled. Both stammer out a greeting to me. Embarrassment probably causes them to make their quick exit. I hear one of them ask the other if I heard their conversation. These women are what I call church hoppers and preacher groupies. Some of them don't even care if the preacher is married; they just want to be all up in that rarified preacher air. They don't understand that lots of faithful Christian men don't even consider dating women who aren't in the kingdom of God. Those brothers usually date women they'd consider for marriage.

I head back to the lobby and Usher Gray. Now that I have bladder relief, I'm ready to respond to his smart remark. He's standing in a corner of the lobby, talking with his pal, Usher Fenton. I start in their direction, and then, realize I'm being both petty and silly. I mentally scold myself.

"This isn't a Christian attitude. Who am I to judge those ladies in the restroom when I'm rushing to get on the usher's nerves before I go back into the worship service? Please forgive me, Lord." I stop, turn, and walk to the door of the auditorium. Usher Gray jerks his box-shaped head around in time to see me reach for the door handle.

"Hold it, Sister NikkiMac! You can't go in now, we're about to have communion. The brothers are serving the bread and fruit of the vine; there is no walking at this time. You can wait out here. The brothers will serve you communion when they come out." It's not what he says, but the way he says it and the glee on his face. That's what gets under my skin. While he's correct that we respect the Lord's remembrance by restricting movement during communion, I feel like he gets his rocks off because he gets to keep me out of the auditorium.

"Give me strength, Jesus," I whisper softly.

"Excuse me; did you say something to me?" Usher Gray advances, while Usher Fenton reaches for his arm. I take a deep breath, rear my shoulders back, and stretch to my maximum height. I'm loading for bear, Usher Gray Bear. I look up into his dark brown eyes before I speak.

"Back up off me, Satan. By the way, your fly is unzipped. What in the world have you been *doing* out here?"

I fake a sweet smile and move away. Both men look down at Usher Gray's crotch to see that I'm right. Brother Gray hastily grabs for his zipper. Brother Fenton rapidly turns his head away and opens the door for the brothers coming out of the auditorium. They serve me communion, and I return to my seat. I feel a little smug and a little guilty, but I'm happy I didn't fully "go off" verbally on Usher Gray. That would have been so wrong. I've got to learn to ignore his bullying behavior.

Brother Leethan leads us in *It Is Well With My Soul*. After we sing the last note, something happens.

"Boom!"

"Whoomp!"

There's thunderous noise outside! Lights blink. Some people make noises of shock and panic. At first, I instinctively duck and protect my head with my arms. Then my nosiness kicks in and I look around to see if someone got shot or something. Sister Carolina is on her butt on the floor; I see her fat legs and sensible pumps. She must have been coming into the auditorium at the time of the big sound, gotten startled by the noise, and fallen. Two ushers rush to her aid and ask if she's alright. She doesn't respond; she just sits there with her legs out, looking like a chubby rag doll. The men slowly help her to her feet. The lights continue to blink. Poppa Pace grabs his cell phone and goes outside. He quickly returns and talks to our minister. Then Brother Johnson talks to us.

"Brothers and sisters, Brother Pace contacted Public Service. The loud sounds we heard came from a transformer that blew. The company has an emergency repair crew on its way right now. Power is out on this block, but we are not in any danger here. So, let us continue to worship, because God is still in this place. We know He has all authority and power. Amen?"

"Amen!" is our reply.

"Christians and visitors, we've got God's daylight to see by. We can get by without the microphone system, I'll just speak louder!"

"Amen, Brother Johnson!"

"If a soul wants to be baptized before, during, or after my sermon, we've got enough daylight to do that! Am I right about it?"

"You are so right, Brother Johnson!"

"Preach, man!"

"I know I'm not the song leader, but come on and sing with me, church!" Brother Johnson begins *Leaning On The Everlasting Arms* and we soulfully sing along. The words of the hymn encourage and reassure me. I'm all into it, my eyes closed, my head thrown back, belting out the alto part of the song. Suddenly I feel a tap on my shoulder; I open my eyes and look at Usher Gray's mischievous expression.

"Sister NikkiMac, you need to move over. You have guests at the door who want to sit next to you."

I'm puzzled, but I scoot over, and then turn to see who my unexpected guests are. It's Angeleese, with her five children trailing behind her. Usher Gray leads them in. On her way down the aisle, Angeleese pauses at each pew and makes the sign of the cross. I guess she thinks she's in another kind of church. The children imitate their mom. This line of six people steps, stops, and crosses themselves all the way to where I'm sitting. I can't help but smile. I reach out to hug Angeleese when she sits next to me. Jacee and Brother Luke move over, so there's plenty of room for Angeleese, Scooter, Ziggy, Cha-Cha, Mookie, and Shay Shay. The children wave at me. We all settle as Brother Johnson steps into the pulpit.

"Good morning to everyone. It's a blessing to be in the Lord's house this day. I'm happy to be with you and to have another chance to worship God in spirit and in truth. How appropriate that we temporarily have no electric power and that it's darker than usual in here. I say that because my sermon today is about haunting, and most stories about haunted houses have darkness as the environment." Brother Johnson has my attention, I am curious to see where he's going with haunting in the context.

"Please turn in your Bibles to Matthew chapter 12, verses 43 through

45. Jesus tells a parable about a man with an unclean spirit. The spirit haunts the man's house, the house being the man himself. When the evil spirit comes out of the man, Christ tells us that the unclean spirit travels about, trying to find rest. The spirit is unsuccessful at finding rest, so he decides to go back to his former house, gets there, and finds it empty and all cleaned and dressed up. What does this unclean spirit do? He rounds up seven other spirits worse than him and they all move into the clean house. The poor house, the man, is now in worse shape than he was at first! What learning can we take from this parable? How can you determine whether or not you live in a haunted house? First, if you want to reform, you must do more than rid yourself of evil. You have to replace the evil with good, and it has to be good according to God's will. Otherwise, you will be worse off than you were at the start."

"Say so, preacher!"

"Teach, brother!"

"Let me give a practical example; I'm not picking on you, sisters, you know I love and respect you all, but this is my first thought. Let's say you are a sister whose house is haunted by the sin of fornication. You become convicted and repent of that sin, thereby cleaning your house of that fornicating spirit. But, you don't replace that unclean spirit with something positive, you just avoid fornication. However, you *do* start judging others who you suspect are fornicating. You *do* start envying the happily married sisters. You *do* start calling every friendly single brother a dog because he smiles at you and other women. You *do* become a very negative member of the congregation. You *do* begin to overeat to fill the void left when you stopped committing fornication. You *do* shut yourself off from fellow Christians more and more. You *do* start thinking that God has no idea of your loneliness. Church, isn't that an example of seven unclean spirits?"

"Yes, Preacher Johnson, that's seven!"

"Amen! Teach, Brother Johnson!"

"Good point, brother!"

"That's right, make it plain!"

I have to admit that Brother Johnson is stepping on my toes. From the response of the audience, I'm not the only one affected. Sister Batts, always the extremist, waves her hands in the air and stomps her feet.

"We invite these unclean spirits when we fail to replace discarded evil with good. We invite the haunting. Also, you live in a haunted house when you try to be on the fence about your faith. A third point, and this was in my earlier example, you live in a haunted house when you have a negative spirit."

"I know that's right!"

"Amen! Amen!"

Angeleese has been listening closely. Except for asking me to find the scriptures mentioned at the beginning of the sermon, she has given the preacher her full attention. A couple of her children repeat the responses of the audience. It's sweet.

Brother Johnson continues. "A house can be filled, but still be empty. It can be empty of acceptance, trust, shared concern, love, kindness, Christian teaching. Always remember that a life without Christ is terribly empty, no matter how much worldly power, wealth, and prestige one may have. I pose this question to you. Do you live in a haunted house? Do you live in a vacant house? I beseech you to fill your life with something positive. Fill it with the positive influence of the gospel. Allow Jesus Christ, the Son of God, to live in your house. He lives in the believer's body through and by God's Holy Spirit. If you repent of your sins, confess Jesus as God's Son, and submit to baptism, you will be added to the kingdom of God. As we sing this song, I urge you to come to Jesus. Welcome Him into your house. Won't you come today?"

We stand for the invitation song. I look at Angeleese to see if she's been persuaded to accept Christ. She whispers, "NikkiMac, I don't want to live in a haunted house. I believe Jesus is the Son of God. I really want to go to heaven when I die. I want my kids to go to heaven, too. But I don't want to go down under that water. I don't even take showers 'cause I don't like to be under the water. I take baths instead. I feel like I can't breathe in all that water; I'm afraid I might drown!" I hold her hand.

"Angeleese, you don't have to be afraid. The baptizing brother tells you when to hold your breath, and you're only under the water for a second. He holds you; he won't let you go. Trust me, it happens really fast."

She looks at me with moist eyes. "NikkiMac, please pray for me and my babies. I'm all they have." It looks like she's trembling a little.

"Angeleese, God loves you and your babies. Listen, I want you to speak with Brother Johnson and Brother Pace today. They'll help you understand about baptism. Promise me you'll talk to them after this service."

"I promise, NikkiMac. Thanks."

The invitation song is over; we all sit down to hear the announcements. I signal Poppa Pace, and he comes to me. "Poppa Pace, Angeleese says she wants to go to heaven, but she's afraid of the baptism process. She has a fear of drowning."

He understands immediately. "Don't worry about it, Daughter NikkiMac. I'll make sure to speak with her right after service. I'll also grab Brother Johnson, he'll counsel her."

"Thanks, Poppa Pace." He returns to his seat next to Cletus, and a bell goes off in my head. Angeleese told me that Cletus is the father of her twins Mookie and Shay Shay. I don't know if she knows that Cletus is a member of the church, but I quickly decide it's neither my place nor the right time to say anything about it. Just then, we hear another loud sound; and the power is back on.

"Hallelujah!"

"Praise the Lord!"

Brother Martin begins today's announcements. "There are only a few announcements today."

"Amen!" a teenager says, but the look of embarrassment on her face tells me she meant to say it in her mind, not aloud. Her mother sends the young lady a look of warning.

"As I was saying," a stern-looking Brother Martin continues, "the ushers request that members refrain from letting babies play with our hand fans. Look at this one, the wooden stick is torn off." He waves the disabled fan for all to see. "I'd be ashamed to give this to a visitor. Please bring a suitable item for your baby to play with so we don't misuse the church property."

"Amen, brother!"

"Please do not park in the minister's designated parking space. It is so labeled. If your name is not Brother Obadiah Johnson or you are not driving his car, you should not park in that space. Come on, people, let's all do what's right. We don't pay him enough for all the work he does, the least we can do is make sure he doesn't have to search for a parking space when he gets here." Some scattered sounds of agreement ring out.

"This announcement is for the students who made the honor roll at school last marking period. We want to recognize and encourage you for your wonderful effort. In two weeks, we will have a brief ceremony to award you with refreshments and achievement certificates. But remember, you must bring in and show your report card to our youth leader. Last year, a student received accolades at three ceremonies before we found out that he hadn't made the honor roll at all. Instead, he was spending more time in the principal's office than in class! That was dishonest, certainly not Christian behavior. Am I right, church?"

"That's right, brother."

"Tell it, Brother Martin!"

"We believe in education and, thankfully, the majority of our young people here do a fine job of representing the church in their schools. Am I right about it?"

"Yes, brother!"

"That's right!"

"Finally, we see some obvious texting during the services. In fact, one person was seen whispering into a cell phone during service. Please, we don't want to single you out and embarrass you, but your cell phones and other gadgets should not be used during worship. If for emergency reasons you just have to receive a call while you're here, put your phone on vibrate mode so it doesn't disturb our service. You can then go outside and take the call."

As soon as Brother Martin finishes this statement, a ring tone of rap music blasts. As usual, the person in possession of the ringing cell phone looks around with surprise. He can't find and turn off the gadget before the second or third ring sequence flies out into the air. The offender blushes, gets up, and fumbles with the cell phone while hastily leaving the auditorium.

Brother Martin shakes his head from side to side. "Those are the announcements for today. Brother Adam Greene will offer closing prayer. Please stand, and let's bow our heads in reverence to God." I look for the women I overheard in the restroom; they must be about to swoon, because Adam is strolling his way down the aisle towards the pulpit.

"Please pray with me. Heavenly Father, holy is your name. Thank you for your mercy and your grace. Thank you for allowing us to worship in spirit and truth today. Please help us keep Your word in our hearts and apply it to our lives. Please continue to bless us in the ways we need blessing. We offer You all glory and praise. In the name of Jesus Christ we pray. Amen."

The church says "Amen." People begin shaking hands and talking. Out of the corner of my eye, I catch Darius Muse trying to get my attention, but I'm not yet ready to do more than the hi-and-goodbye thing with him. I turn to the children and give each a hug, then do the same to their mother. Soon, Poppa Pace appears.

"Miss Angeleese, Brother Johnson and I would like to speak with you for a few minutes. We are honored that you and your children are here with us today. Come on and walk with me to Brother Johnson's office. Sister NikkiMac will take your children to the church nursery. The sisters there will be on duty for at least the next thirty minutes. They'll take care of your children for you."

Angeleese turns to her children. "Now, you all be good. Mommy will come and get you in a little while. You know how I want you to behave, right?" Four of them nod silently.

"Yes, Momma!" Little Cha-Cha snaps her fingers and bops her head like it is all good with her. The children follow me; Angeleese walks with Poppa Pace. I want to go with Angeleese and Poppa Pace, but after I take the children to the nursery, I have to attend an Education Committee meeting. Jacee and I both serve on the committee; she's in the classroom when I enter. We embrace warmly.

"Hello, NikkiMac. How are you? I called you last night but I didn't leave a message."

"Hi Jacee, What's up with that? You usually fill my answering machine with your babbling, always trying to use up my tape cassette."

"I keep telling you to come out of the Stone Age and get voice mail." We both laugh, and then embrace again. I miss being with her.

"Seriously, NikkiMac, I need to talk to you. I'm having some concerns about Brother Luke." She looks quite serious, so I give her my full attention.

"We have a few minutes before the other committee members get here. Give me the short version, Jacee."

"Brother Luke, Lawrence is his first name, is beginning to crowd me. Don't get me wrong, I enjoy having the attention of a Christian guy. You know I don't date men who are not in the church. However, Lawrence shows signs of being a control freak. He takes up so much of my free time that I struggle to make time for my friends and family. It's like he wants me all to himself."

"Jacee, does he tell you not to interact with your friends and family?"

"No, but lately he makes plans for us without asking me first. I'm talking about dates for the movies, dinner, shows, and such. They really are nice plans, but he sets them up without my input, then tells me what they are, where we're scheduled to be, and when we're scheduled to be there. When I tell him I have something else scheduled: to see you, my family, or someone else, Lawrence tries to run a guilt trip on me. He tells me he just wants to make me happy and that most women would be thrilled to have a man who puts forth effort to show that they care."

"Is he your man, Jacee?"

She raises both arms in exasperation, her palms face upward. "That's another thing, NikkiMac; I never told Lawrence that he was my man. As far as I'm concerned, we are still getting to know each other. I've never even let him kiss me, so how can he think he's my man?"

"Jacee, I've known you since elementary school, and you've never had a problem speaking your mind. Did you tell Lawrence he's pushing too hard and fast?"

"Not yet, NikkiMac. I don't want to hurt his feelings, but I'm starting to resent his pushiness."

"Jacee, his pushiness is what I call a *tell*: it's a warning of what's really going on as well as what is to come. Inch by inch, Lawrence is taking over. Any man who tries to isolate you from the supportive people who were in your life before he came along is a scary guy! Think about this, it's only been a couple of months and he's claiming you without your consent. Maybe he thinks you're desperate. Some church men think sisters in their forties and older will put up with anything in order to catch and marry an eligible Christian man. Some believe we're all hard up."

"I hear what you're saying, NikkiMac. But I can say that Lawrence hasn't pressured me for sex, so fornication isn't an issue for us."

"Jacee, my dear sister, don't think his controlling behavior will stop at sexual intimacy. Don't let him suck your essence from you. Please know I'm not a hater; I just love you so much that I want what's best for you. Know this: any man who tries to think for a grown woman is not good for that woman."

The excess moisture in Jacee's eyes is evident. I wrap my arm around her shoulders. First one, and then three other members of the committee enter the classroom. Jacee quickly composes herself and we agree to continue this conversation after evening worship service. Thankfully, the meeting is short, just the way I like it. We put the finishing touches on our Vacation Bible School activities, have prayer, and dismiss. Jacee and I walk to the parking lot together.

"NikkiMac, let's meet at Diamonds Diner after evening worship service. We can talk there and have some dessert."

"That's cool with me; I love their cheesecake." We reach her car and see Brother Luke leaning against the passenger side door. Jacee acts surprised to see him.

"Hey Jacee, I was wondering where you went. Are you ready? We have lunch reservations at the airport restaurant." Brother Luke looks a little irritated.

"What? I didn't know we had plans for today. Anyway, I told you I had an Education Committee meeting after morning service." Lawrence acts like he doesn't notice me standing right next to Jacee, so I make him notice.

"Hello, Brother Luke. What's the matter, you can't speak? Cat got your tongue?"

"Oh, hello, Sister NikkiMac, I'm sorry for not speaking. I'm just trying to get Jacee fed. Uh, did I just hear you two make a date for tonight?" He looks concerned.

"Yes, Lawrence, NikkiMac and I have something to discuss. Is that a problem for you?"

"Well, Jacee, I thought I'd take you to that movie you've been eager to see. I already have the tickets." Now, I see the behavior that concerns Jacee.

"Lawrence, we can go to lunch now, but tonight I need to spend time with NikkiMac." Jacee sounds like she's on the verge of annoyance.

"Well, maybe I can join you two ladies tonight at the diner, my treat. It will be our first threesome."

He smiles a little too brightly for my comfort. I think, "Nobody invited your controlling self. You're the *topic* of tonight's conversation!" I make a "Do you want me to handle this?" expression to Jacee, so she steps it up.

"Look, Lawrence. It's just me and NikkiMac tonight." His expression tries to mask what he's feeling, but for a second I see anger cross his face, all up in the eyebrow area. Then his face relaxes. Another bit of information for my mental file.

Brother Lawrence Luke regroups. "Okay, Jacee, I'll meet you in ten minutes at Diamonds Diner." He doesn't say anything to me, but gives me a piercing look. Then he walks away.

Jacee hugs me as I declare, "We will work it out, my sister." I watch Jacee drive off and turn to walk to my car. I wave at fellow Christians who are leaving the parking lot.

"NikkiMac, I want to thank you!" It's Angeleese and her posse of children. "Girl, that Brother Pace is so nice! So is your minister. They talked to me about how I can get baptized without drowning. I am going to think about this baptism thing. But NikkiMac, I think I saw somebody in church that looked like a cleaned-up Cletus. Was that him?"

"Yes, Angeleese, Cletus was at church today."

"Why is he coming to church, NikkiMac? He didn't used to come to church before, did he?"

"Cletus is a member of the church now, Angeleese. He's been baptized and he comes to church on a regular basis."

She looks stunned and confused. "Cletus got baptized and comes to church on the regular?" I can imagine the gears in her brain struggling to turn this news into reality for sweet but simple Angeleese. "Wow! That sure is a lot to think on." Her children begin to get restless. "Okay, my babies, let's go home so I can fix you some lunch. How about hot dogs and beans?"

"Yay, yay, yay! Hot dogs and beans today!" Ziggy starts the chant and the four other children join in. Angeleese chuckles. They lead their mother away while they march and chant their hot dog and beans ditty. I can't help but smile.

Chapter 20   Sister Keke's Funeral

Sister Keke Lewis looks likes she's asleep, but when I touch her hands, they are cold and hard. Her red hair is styled in a large bouffant of which she'd be proud. The casket is open only up to a little past her folded hands, so I can't tell if she's fully dressed in one of her usual stretchy outfits. The funeral home got her makeup correct in the sense that there's lots of it on Keke's face. Someone has applied so much foundation and powder that she almost appears to be a white female. Her face looks relaxed and pretty, though. Ever since the funerals for my parents, I attempt to avoid these affairs. I started not to attend this one, but Poppa Pace spoke with me about this.

"Daughter NikkiMac, the sister has very little family that we know of. Her church family should come out and show our love and support. The funeral is on Saturday, so it's not a work day for you. Attend if you can."

His words touched me, so here I am. Jacee didn't come with me. While I try to avoid funerals, Jacee is phobic about them. She says that after attending a funeral, she dreams about corpses for weeks. I often tell her there's one funeral she'll grace with her physical presence, although she won't know she's there. Every time I tease her this way, she pops me and almost cusses.

I finish viewing Sister Keke's body and return to my seat. The church auditorium is almost half full. Only one pew on the right is occupied by Keke's family. Two young ladies cry softly. They look alike, but neither of them resembles Sister Keke, yet they're reacting as if they just lost their mother. Three elderly women look cheerless and weary. An aged man sits at the end of the pew with his walker at the side. Only these six people sit in the area designated for family, so I'm glad I came to pay my respects. Poppa Pace was on point, as usual. Most of the attendees I recognize as members of our congregation. However, there are several men who don't look familiar. A couple of them are dressed in flashy throwback outfits, but they aren't bad-looking guys. Their expressions reveal they are taking this quite hard; they must be close to Sister Keke. I wonder why they aren't sitting with the family. I don't say this out loud, but I don't have to. I'm sitting next to Sister Melody, who turns out to be the *Queen of Whispers and Complaints* for today.

"Hmm, I wonder who some of these men are. A couple of them sure are fine! Do you suppose they're from Sister Keke's family? If they are, they should be sitting with the rest of the family." Sister Melody's excitement at the prospect of being admired by new men is palpable. I try to ignore her, but she doesn't notice.

"Sister NikkiMac, I wonder why they don't let Brother Vincent lead the songs. He's definitely our best song leader. The brother they have listed in this funeral program just drags the songs. I know this is a funeral, but we need to be a little upbeat to celebrate her life."

"Sister Melody, I don't know. I didn't plan the funeral." I'm trying hard not to allow Melody to get on my last nerve.

"Sister NikkiMac, don't you think they could have done a better job on these funeral programs? They are kind of tacky." I give no response. Thankfully, the funeral director and his assistant solemnly walk forward. They direct the family to take a final view of Sister Keke before the casket is closed. They do so, and the two young ladies cry more loudly and painfully. The four older family members wipe their damp eyes with handkerchiefs and hold on to each other as they take a last look. Then, they all slowly return to their seats. The director rearranges a satin pillow near Keke's face. He inserts a handle into a mechanism in the casket, and winds her upper body from a slight incline to a flat position. It's weird to see her head lower; it's almost like she's doing it on her own. His assistant removes the brass banker's lamp from the open casket. The funeral director folds the lovely pastel pink satin liner into the casket, gently covers Keke's face, and tenderly closes the coffin. His partner places a lovely floral arrangement over the top half that was once open. They work in perfect synchronization. It's seamless. We see Sister Keke no more; just a shiny pink delicately accented steel casket, surrounded by flowers.

Sister Melody lets me know why. "Sister NikkiMac, you see that he closes the coffin before the funeral service starts, don't you? Oh yes, he has to. The last time the coffin was left open during a funeral here, family members kept going up to it all during the program. They talked to the body like it could hear. People stared at the deceased all through the service. Then, when the director moved to close the lid before the recessional, kinfolk jumped up and tried to stop him. They did not want to see him close the lid on their loved one. I guess it was too final for them after the service. It was a real hootenanny up in here! So, this funeral director always has the family get their last look before the program begins, just in case folks get too worked up later." Sister Melody wears the satisfied expression of someone who has just dropped some deep knowledge on a lowly peon.

Suddenly, Brother Lawrence Luke rushes up front, lays his head on the closed casket, and wails sorrowfully. Many of us look surprised. Sister Melody elbows me and whispers, "What's up with that? Isn't he your girl Jacee's man? Why is he all broke down over a sister he hardly knows?" I don't know what to think or say, but even if I did, I wouldn't say it to Melody. Brother Luke backs away from the coffin and turns to go back to his seat. As he passes by, he glances at me and quickly looks away. His grief appears to be sincere, so his tears must not be crocodile tears. This is more info for my mental file.

Brother Johnson enters the pulpit to address the group. "We are here today to celebrate the home going of our dear Sister Keke Lewis. Thank you all for coming to support the family. Our dear sister died in the Lord, and for that we are joyful. In Revelation chapter 14, verse 13, we learn that those who die in the Lord are blessed, that they are at rest, and that the good they have done in this life counts for them. We will miss Sister Keke, but we believe we'll see her and the other departed saints when we all meet in heaven. And now, Brother Leethan will lead us in a hymn."

The song leader begins *Victory In Jesus*. Sister Melody sings in a loud falsetto that she probably thinks is operatic, but to me, it's eerie and comical. She sounds like the cackling, broomstick-riding witch in a fairy tale. My victory for today will be to survive her vocals for the duration of this funeral. Brother Dexter leads us in the reading of the Old Testament selection, Psalm 23. Brother Elton follows with the New Testament selection, Revelation chapter 21, verse 4. Both of these scripture readings are reassuring to me. I look up from my Bible to see Brother Adam Greene in the pulpit.

"Good morning. Please bow with me in a prayer of comfort. Heavenly Father, thank you for giving us Sister Keke. She was blessed by you with a kind and humble spirit. She didn't say much, but you gave her the gift of listening, and so we were blessed by that. Please be with her family and her Christian family. Help ease our sadness of missing her physical presence, for we know she's in a better place. A place where the faithful go when You call them to their rest. Help us live in a way that we too can be in that place of rest when you call us from this earth. Then, at the Day of Judgment, we will be with and praise You forevermore. We pray in the name of Jesus. Amen."

Brother Leethan comes forward to lead us in *What A Friend We Have in Jesus*. Sister Melody creates her own solo part. She is a trip, a songstress in her own mind.

Sisters Lolah and Lelah Maze march to the front of the room and go to the microphone near the casket. Lolah reads some of the sympathy cards that were selected earlier by the family. Lelah hands each card to her sister and holds it after it is read. This catches the attention of Sister Melody. "Why do both of them have to be up there? Only one of them is reading; the other one doesn't even talk half of the time. Sister Lolah can't talk and hold cards at the same time?" I'm getting a little tired of Melody and I haven't allowed my longsuffering to kick in yet, so I respond.

"Sister Melody, would you please be quiet? I am trying to listen."

She stiffens, bugs her eyes, and looks shocked. "You don't have to get an attitude, Sister NikkiMac. All that is not even called for!" She moves over to put some distance between the two of us. That's fine with me.

Sister Lolah reads the obituary from the program. We read along silently. It's only a couple of paragraphs. Sister Keke's date of birth is listed; I compute that she's about ten years older than me. Her late parents' names are listed; it appears the four elderly people sitting in the family area here are her aunts and an uncle. The obituary names two foster children; they must be the two young ladies. It appears they have aged out of foster care, but Keke must have raised them at some point in their lives. After reading the obituary, Sisters Lolah and Lelah march back to their seats. Brother Johnson asks if anyone wants to offer remarks about Sister Keke. I didn't get to know her that well, so I don't intend to walk over the microphone. Frankly, I'm surprised when five of the unfamiliar men, followed by Poppa Pace, get up and head for the front.

The first speaker looks distinguished. He's probably in his sixties. He clears his throat and begins, "I knew Keke long ago, before she became a church woman. She lived a different life then, but she always had a good heart and a kind word for me. Not too long ago, word came to me that she was sick. I returned to Trenton, asked around, and found out she had already passed. I'm so sorry I did not get a chance to see her sweet smile one more time. I offer my condolences to her family."

As he walks away from the microphone, Sister Melody looks at me and stretches her eyes wide. I think she wants to move back over so she can comment, but I slowly shake my head from side to side to warn her to stay where she sits. Melody pouts at me.

The second man speaks, "Giving an honor to God. I used to go to a church, but that's not where I met lovely Keke. I just want to say that when we met up back in the day, she always treated me fairly; she never tried to cheat me. I did not know she was sick; although I hadn't seen her for awhile. She was a sweet lady." He bows his head and sadly walks away from the microphone.

The next man blows his nose, and then puts his tissue in his pocket. "I saw Keke in the hospital about a month ago. She let me know she was real bad off and would probably not be around much longer. But she wasn't upset, and that really got to me. She actually comforted me when I started crying. She said she had made her peace with God and had been faithful in the church here since her repentance from her old life. She still looked good, so for a while, I thought she was pulling my leg. Then, right before I left, she handed me a tract about the church and begged me to get right with God soon. I promised her I would, and I always keep my word. I will be here next Sunday morning. My first reason for that is to keep my word to Keke. The second reason is to see how this faith totally changed Keke's lifestyle." His remarks elicit strong audience response.

"Amen!"

"Praise the Lord!"

"Come to Jesus!"

The next two men make similar positive remarks about Sister Keke. I bet I'm not the only person who wonders what past connection these guys have with the deceased. Whatever it is, they hold her in high regard.

When I die, it would be nice to have people give such a kind testimony about me. I probably won't know about the accolades, but the good words would certainly comfort my remaining loved ones.

Poppa Pace is the final person to address this remarks segment. "It was a pleasure to know Sister Keke Lewis. I met her many years ago; before she was my sister in Christ, so I got to see the way God changed her life. Sister Keke and I did not interact in a business sense, but we did have many conversations about earthly life, eternal life, and heaven. Her personality was always lovable; she just needed to make a major change in her livelihood. Our Father enabled her to make that change. She left one occupation and found a more appropriate one. Just as God forgave our sins, He forgave Sister Keke, and she never looked back. She became a quiet worker in the kingdom. Whenever she did a kindness for someone, she never tooted her own horn about it. Her lovely girls she helped raise are evidence of her caring nature. Today at her service, you heard a gentleman speak about coming to church to keep his promise to Sister Keke. We will miss her, but she has earned her rest. If we also live faithfully until death, we will see her on the other side." He walks to the family to offer comforting words and supportive embraces. Brother Leethan steps forward and leads *God Will Take Care Of You.*

Brother Johnson begins the eulogy. "Sister Keke knew her illness was progressing rapidly, and that the doctors felt they could do no more for her other than palliative care. Yet, she believed that God could cure her, if it was His will. She knew that He had the power to overrule the doctors as well as the cancer. She decided she was going to trust in His will and accept whatever fate God had for her. She asked me to share her story at her home going service because she thought it might encourage others and strengthen their faith in the power of God. She was thinking of others even as she approached her end on this earth. So, I am honoring her wish, and I pray you will hear her story with open and honest hearts." He clears his throat and looks solemnly at the audience. Sister Melody starts to slide my way, but I quickly block her proximity with my oversized designer purse.

"Sister Keke wanted you to know some facts about her life. For five years, she worked as a female escort, which means she received money for her company and other services. Sister Keke wanted me to be more specific in my telling you about her occupation, but I told her I would have to do some editing for a church service. Know this, her objective in asking me to tell you this was not to brag or sensationalize. Rather, it was to allow the hearers to see the sharp contrast between her former life and her new life in the church. She hoped to offer encouragement to people who think their lives are so bad that God cannot transform them. Is there anything too hard for God?"

Poppa Pace and only a few others respond, "No, brother! Nothing is too hard for God!" I guess the majority of the audience is too stunned to say anything. For most of us, this is an unusual twist on a funeral service.

Brother Johnson continues, "Based on what the clients desired, Sister Keke's manager would set up dates for her and the other escorts. They were provided a menu of services with varying fees. The more extensive the service was, the more expensive the cost. The escorts were required to give part of their earnings to the manager. Initially, Sister Keke didn't see anything wrong with her line of work. It wasn't forced upon her, she chose it. She found it exciting and profitable. Because her emphasis was on companionship and accompanying clients to various social and business events, she felt she was assisting her clients."

I am on the verge of my seat, looking directly at our minister, but out of the corner of my eye, I detect movement. Some of the men who earlier gave positive remarks about Sister Keke are walking out of the auditorium. All of them, actually, except for the one who promised Keke he'd come to church. Maybe the rest are embarrassed about Sister Keke's post-life candor. She outed them, but not for a bad reason. Maybe they're married or ashamed because they used to pay for female companionship. Anyway, they leave. For about a full minute, it's so quiet in the auditorium that you could hear a mouse tinkle on cotton. I figure everyone is processing what Brother Johnson has just said. It's not every day that your minister prefaces a eulogy with a racy confession. Then, the whispers begin.

"What did Brother Johnson say?"

"What kind of dating services is he talking about?"

"Is this about sex?"

"Why are those men leaving? Are they her old clients? You heard what they said earlier!"

"Sister Keke used to be a prostitute? That's a shame before the Lord!"

"What crazy kind of funeral is this?"

Brother Johnson speaks in a strong voice. "I hear murmuring, but I want you to listen. Consider the words of Jesus Christ in Matthew chapter 21, verses 31 through 32. There is mercy for any sinner who comes to repentance. Think about your past sins, and don't judge. Be thankful for God's grace in your life, and for how He is changing you. Be thankful for how God changed Sister Keke in time for her to live many years in the kingdom of God. You see, over time Sister Keke began to question herself about her job. That's the self confrontation I preach to you about. At first, she rationalized that her line of work was levels above streetwalker work. She felt she dressed better; she enjoyed the flashy clothes encouraged by her manager. When she worked, she was picked up at her nice apartment or was met by her clients at classy establishments. Yet, her mind began to change. She wasn't raised in a religious home, but that itch in her mind would not go away. This reminds me of Acts chapter 17, verses 26 and 27. God placed in mankind the desire to search after Him. Sister Keke began her search, and so the escort work became harder to rationalize. Thankfully, she met some Christians who were canvassing neighborhoods in an evangelistic effort. She studied with them, left that lifestyle, and soon after was baptized into Christ."

"Praise the Lord!"

"Thank you, Jesus!"

"I'm thankful she turned to Jesus. I'm also thankful for that type of door-to-door evangelism. We don't do as much of that type of evangelism these days. Sometimes I think we get too comfortable in our cushioned church seats. But twenty or thirty years ago, we'd canvass neighborhoods, street by street. Gospel tracts would be distributed; Bible classes would be scheduled and conducted in people's homes. The church went out to the streets to get the word of God out to people in sin. Brother Pace and Brother Kelsey, you remember those days, don't you?"

"I sure do, Brother Johnson," Poppa Pace responds. Brother Kelsey, who surprisingly, is awake, nods his head in affirmation.

"Well, I've told you Sister Keke's story. I've told you why she wanted it heard. Now, let me tell you the victory in all this. Sister Keke is just asleep. She has transitioned to the next part of eternal life. Open your

Bibles again. Look at First Thessalonians chapter 4, verses 13 through 18."

Around the room, delicate Bible pages turn; they make a soft rustling sound. I notice Brother Kelsey repeatedly touch his right index finger to his tongue to wet it before he uses it to turn the thin pages of his Bible. He once told me this makes the pages easier to turn. As far as I can tell, only the older members do this. We younger members have been educated to the max about the plethora of germs that live on our fingers. This procedure doesn't seem to bother our seniors, though. I think they are made of stronger stock than the younger generations.

"This passage in First Thessalonians informs us that we have hope, because when Jesus comes, those who died in faith will rise from their sleep. They will meet the Lord in the sky and ultimately be in heaven praising God and rejoicing throughout eternity. What can be more victorious than that? Sister Keke will be able to claim her victory in Christ. We should all strive for the same. So, let us not be overcome with sorrow, for God has called a faithful servant home. If you have not been baptized into Christ for the forgiveness of your sins, you need to do what Sister Keke did one day many years ago. Come, get right with God. That way, you'll be ready when your eyes are closed at the end of your earthly life."

"Amen!"

"Hallelujah!"

"Praise God!"

Brother Johnson proceeds to offer an invitation to those who have not been added to the body of Christ. We sing a song of encouragement, *Are You Washed In The Blood*. No one comes forth, but perhaps someone has been moved to at least think about obtaining salvation. The funeral director asks, "May I have a few young ladies to carry the flowers outside?" The twins, Sisters Lolah and Lelah Maze, Sister Longstreet, Sister Batts, and Sister Pearl quickly go forward. The funeral director places a floral arrangement in each of their hands, and the ladies walk toward the auditorium doors and the front exit.

Sister Melody notices that one more floral arrangement is left. She announces loudly, "Excuse me, Sister NikkiMac; I need to get past you to give my assistance with the flowers." She makes a big show of stepping over me in the pew. That chicklet always has to be seen and heard. At first I feel like tripping her, but realize that would not be the righteous thing to do. I tuck my feet in under the seat to make it easier for her to pass by. As she does her slow celebrity walk out with the last of the flowers, the director and his assistant signal us to stand. Brother Johnson begins quoting John chapter 11, verses 25 and 26, as he walks toward the auditorium doors. Following Brother Johnson, the pallbearers escort the casket up the aisle. The family follows the casket outside to the waiting hearse and funeral car for the family. We exit row by row from the front to the rear. Outside, the family members get seated in the car behind the hearse. The casket and flowers are loaded into the back of the hearse. Many people stand around speaking to each other.

"Girl, I haven't seen you since that funeral here two years ago. Do you still live in Trenton?"

"About the only occasions I see people who attended Trenton Central High School with me are at funerals. We need to get together for some happy occasions!"

"What was that all about? I have never been to a funeral with so much excitement and drama!"

"I don't care what Sister Keke wanted us to know about her life as an escort. All I know is that she seemed to be a sweet soul. I wish I had taken the time to know her better."

I make no comment as I hear these remarks, because I am looking for Brother Luke. I don't see him in the crowd, but I do see Boopy, the former drinking buddy of Cletus. He is standing outside the church gate, weaving slightly, and solemnly saluting the funeral procession as it heads for the cemetery. I'll bet Sister Keke would have loved to see that salute. She would have gotten a kick out of it.

Chapter 21   Drifting, Sifting, Holding On

Life is good. I bask in the glow of our Sunday morning service. Brother Vincent leads a stirring song service. Poppa Pace is taking me to the diner for lunch later on. Brother Adam Greene's sermon is encouraging; several points of his message resonate in my mind.

"Brothers and sisters, are you wandering away? Are you paying close attention to where you are on the salvation road? Are you staying close to God? Hebrews chapter 2, verse 1 is a strong reminder for us to concentrate on the sound doctrine we have heard, so we don't let it get away from us. Second Peter chapter 3, verse 18 tells us we must continue to grow in both grace and in the knowledge of Jesus. This suggests an intimacy that is built by obedience to God's commands, an active prayer life, and consistent attention to the scriptures. I have some questions I want you to consider. You don't have to raise your hand or answer aloud; this is for self confrontation."

Jacee smiles at me. She's back in her seat next to me, minus Brother Luke. She told me we'd discuss this after evening service. I return the smile and grab my pen, because I definitely need to write Brother Adam Greene's sermon questions in my notes.

"Do you have less of a desire to study and meditate on the word of God?"

I study the Sunday School lesson for about fifteen minutes on Saturday nights. Our adult Sunday School class uses a Bible-based lesson book. I feel somewhat guilty, because I don't do daily Bible reading. I do thank God during the day and evening, especially when I do what's right. I recognize that my goodness comes from Him.

"Do you have less desire to attend worship services?"

I attend services regularly; it's become one of my good habits. I recognize the need to be here for worship services and classes.

"Do you have less interest in taking the gospel to others?"

This is a weak area for me. I occasionally invite people to come and hear the gospel, but if they don't accept, I usually don't invite them again. I allow their lack of interest to shut me down.

"Does your conversation on your job include the Lord, whenever it can?"

Some of my coworkers take the position that they don't discuss politics or religion in the workplace. Others are religious, but they make church sound more like a social club than a place where God is worshipped. Some talk more about the worldly behaviors of the church members, including the preacher, than anything else. One colleague, Blaine, stunned me when she revealed that her church's married minister had an affair and a child with a single sister in the congregation, and everybody knew about it. When I asked her how she could stay in that church under his leadership, her reply was, "I just listen to him when he stays in the Bible. When he doesn't, I just ignore him. He excuses his dalliance by saying he's only human. Anyway, my whole family has been in that church for years, so I stay. Plus, I love that rocking church instrumental music; it makes me catch the Spirit!" After Blaine told me that, I stopped talking to her about church. Another one of my coworkers has promised to attend our Wednesday night Bible class, though. She became interested because she heard one of Brother Johnson's Sunday morning radio messages.

"Do you spend less time in prayer?"

I actually pray more, because I am growing more aware of when I commit sin.

"Do you feel you don't need as much prayer as you used to need?"

For me, the more prayer, the better.

"Are you getting more pleasure from worldly activities than from godly activities?"

Two words pop into my head: Alex Carson. It's been a while, mostly because I stay busy and avoid being with him. However, I know I'm still vulnerable to our easy, friendly times that lead to playful sex romps.

"Are you less interested in your brothers and sisters in Christ?"

Darius Muse still tries to be friendly when he sees me at church, but all I can manage is a stiff handshake, without looking into his face. I know I'm wrong; he is my brother in Christ. I did say that I forgave him for what he did to me. I could be nicer to Usher Gray. He's actually become more pleasant lately. I'm going to allow the Holy Spirit to work a better attitude in me. The Bible says one can't love God and yet hate one's brother or sister in Christ. Brother Adam Greene is stepping on my toes with this message, but it's good for me; it's good for all of us.

"Church, no matter where you find yourself in your answers to these questions, you are still blessed, because God has allowed you to be here. The blood is still running warm in your veins, so you have the opportunity to submit to God's plan for you. If you are drifting, now is the appointed time for you to recognize it, repent of it, and ask God to forgive and restore you. If you need prayer, come forward and we will pray for you. Drifters, God is sending you a plea through the scriptures. He wants you to stop drifting and stay in Him. Those of you who have not been added to the body of Christ, now is the time. You have heard the gospel, how Christ came to earth and died for the sins of mankind. He was buried and rose on the third day. He is now in heaven interceding for us. When Jesus comes again, it will be to judge mankind and then claim His own. Believe what you have heard, repent of your sins, confess Jesus as the Son of God and be buried with Him in baptism for the forgiveness of your sins. You will be added to the body of Christ, and receive the gift of the Holy Spirit. Remain faithful until death, or until Jesus returns, and heaven will be your eternal home. As we stand to sing a song of invitation, please come to Jesus now."

Brother Vincent starts *I'll Be List'ning* and we all join in heartily. Brother Greene moves back and forth across the front pews, then up and down the aisles, gently encouraging people to come to Christ. Baby Sasha wakes up from her nap and starts clapping her small hands while shouting out what she thinks are the words to the hymn. People smile at her, which encourages her to make even louder noises. Sister Coles holds onto Sasha and sings, as does Brother Coles.

No one accepts the invitation, but a few members ask for prayer that they stay strong in the faith, and not drift away. One member thanks Brother Greene for the message, because it spoke directly to a personal concern of hers. Brother Greene offers prayer on their behalf.

After the prayer, Jacee taps me. "NikkiMac, you notice that Brother Luke isn't here today, don't you?"

"Yes, Jacee, I did notice that." I pause to put my offering envelope in the basket that's carried by an usher.

"He threatened to place his membership at another congregation if I stopped dating him."

"That is downright manipulative, Jacee. It says a lot about his character, though."

Brother Martin has only one announcement, which surprises us. We stand for closing prayer.

"NikkiMac, I've got to head across town to meet my mom. I'll see you tonight." Jacee gives me a hug and leaves. I greet several people, and then see Poppa Pace's smiling face. I get a charge out of the fact that he always looks like he's glad to see me. I feel so blessed to have him as a supportive and faithful father figure. We don't always agree, but he always listens to my concerns and cares about my feelings. I haven't spoken to him about my Alex Carson problem, but I think I will. I just don't want Poppa Pace to be ashamed of me. His daughter Tasha is a big enough problem for him.

"Daughter NikkiMac, I'll be ready in about ten minutes. I have to check and see if all these doors are locked. We don't need to trouble Trenton's finest with another false alarm." He's correct. Although the police have been nice about the false alarms lately, the church shouldn't put other citizen's lives in jeopardy because the police are busy responding to a false burglar alarm. Some members are guilty of exiting through one of the back doors, and not completely closing it. When the alarm is set and the wind jars the unlocked door, a silent alarm is triggered. I make a mental note to get on Usher Gray about that; maybe he can stand by the door at dismissal and prevent folks from exiting there. I think he'd enjoy that power trip.

"No hurry, Poppa Pace. I'll be out here in the lobby. There are a few people still hanging around talking." A group of young teenagers, two girls and three boys, are naively flirting. They are Shaylonda, Chastity, Bobby, Tony, and Curt. Shaylonda makes rhymes using the boys' names, while Chastity grins all over herself.

"Bobby, Bobby, get a hobby. Bobby, Bobby, don't be snobby. Bobby, Bobby, leave this lobby." Both girls burst out giggling. Bobby grins, while his buddies crack up. Shaylonda's not finished.

"Curt, Curt, he wants dessert. Curt, Curt, does he flirt? Curt, Curt, his eyes hurt." More laughter follows this chant. Next, Shaylonda focuses on Tony.

"Tony, Tony, is he phony? Tony, Tony, he's not boney. Tony, Tony, eats baloney." They all laugh good-naturedly. They are so cute, still innocent. I'm happy that these children seem to enjoy being in church together.

My attention is next drawn to Usher Dexter as he escorts Sister Blake to the door. She sees me and calls me over. "I didn't get my hug from you today, Sister NikkiMac. Come here and hug my neck, with your pretty self." I cross the room and embrace this little elderly sister. She always calls me pretty. I guess it's because I try to pay attention to her. I usually make a point of speaking to her. I also pick up her grocery items about once a month.

"That's my girl. You have a blessed afternoon, baby."

"Thank you, Sister Blake. I'll see you at evening service." Usher Dexter continues to the church van with her. I like seeing how gentle and patient he is with our older sister.

Over by the coat rack, a brother who tries to talk to every unmarried sister he sees has Sister Blanche entertained. "Yes, my dear and precious sister in Christ, I decided to come today and get my church on. Good thing I did, because I finally get a chance to say a few words to you. So, can I get those digits?" She looks amused and a little giddy. I hope she doesn't give that pest her phone number. From what I've heard, she'll certainly regret it if she does.

I busy myself with reading the bulletin board announcements until someone puts their hand on my shoulder. This startles me, so I jump, look, and exclaim, "What in the world are you doing in here?" It's stank Tasha Pace. I knock her crusty hand off my shoulder and simultaneously feel my good mood heading south.

"Ain't this a church? Anybody can come here. God is love, haven't you heard, Sister NikkiMac? God loves me, too, even if you don't."

"I know this one thing, Tasha. If you ever come up behind me again and put your dirty paws on me, you will draw back a stub. You'd best believe that."

"NikkiMac, where's the love? Ain't you supposed to love everybody? You sure do love my daddy. I hear you calling him Poppa Pace and him calling you Daughter NikkiMac. I think that stinks."

"Tasha, the only thing that stinks around here is you. Now, what do you want? Your father will be back in a few minutes; we're going out to lunch." Her surprised eye looks even more flabbergasted as she processes this information.

"Oh, so now you got my daddy *feeding* you, huh? NikkiMac, are you trying to move me totally out of the picture?"

"Tasha, you moved yourself away from your father with your trifling lifestyle."

She raises both eyebrows and takes a deep breath before she morphs into a serpent, like in the fairy tales. Her regular eye narrows and her nostrils flare. Tasha hisses, "Well, Miss Thing, I may have a raggedy lifestyle, but I ain't living no lie about who I am. Not like you. Don't think I didn't see you pussyfooting out of Alex Carson's house early in the morning a few months ago. You had on the same clothes coming out that you had on when you went in his house the night before. Oh yes, you know I hang out in the streets; the streets have eyes." She points dramatically at her face, "And these eyes saw you!"

I gasp, and then quickly try to make my face neutral, but my light complexion reddens and betrays me. Tasha wears a triumphant expression.

"Oh, I see I struck a nerve. I was just fishing, trying to see if you would take the bait, and I just saw you suck air. Now, your blushing red face, guilty eyes and quiet mouth tell me I'm right about what you were *doing* in that house with Alex. You may come to church and fool my daddy, but you livin' foul, NikkiMac. You ain't no better than me, and don't you forget that fact."

Just then, Poppa Pace comes into the lobby. He pauses when he sees Tasha, because she usually doesn't come inside the building. "Tasha, why are you here? I told you on the phone last night that I won't give you any money. Now, if you want some groceries, I'll pick some up from the store for you. You can come to the house and I'll give them to you. If you need clothing, I'll let you choose what you need from the church Clothing Bank. I will not give you any cash, because I can't do it in good faith. I believe you'd spend it on getting high."

"Daddy, I'll take the groceries. I don't need the clothes. Thanks for the offer, though. NikkiMac says you and her are going to lunch. Can I go? I know I'm not all dressed up for church like *that one*," she jerks her head in my direction, "but I don't look all that bad today."

I try to figure out what kind of mirror she looked in this morning, because she is tore up from the floor up. Her hair is dyed a burgundy color, and it is standing at attention all over her head. She has on a purple wintertime skirt and an orange summertime blouse. The ensemble is topped off with a dirty brown duster coat. Her feet are sporting black and white low-top sneakers. Her legs and ankles are naked and dirty.

"Tasha, maybe you'll join me another time. I'll have your groceries ready for you after evening church service; you can come by the house and get them." Poppa Pace looks weary, but not the physical kind, more the emotional kind of weary.

"All right then, Daddy. Maybe we can go out to eat at another time, when you don't have your precious fake daughter, NikkiMac, with you. Here's a word to the wise, Daddy. Your sweet little NikkiMac is not as holy as you seem to think she is." Tasha blows a kiss at me, snaps her fingers, does a little spin, and walks her jerky walk in the other direction.

"What's that all about, Daughter NikkiMac?"

"Poppa Pace, half the time I don't know what Tasha is talking about. May we please go eat?" I grab him by the arm and we head for my car. Since he's treating me to the meal, I'm doing the driving. As we leave the parking lot, I notice Tasha in my rear view mirror. She's sticking her tongue out and giving me the finger.

Oblivious to Tasha's obscene gesture, Poppa Pace settles into the passenger seat, and then turns to me. "NikkiMac, perhaps you've noticed that Tasha is growing increasingly jealous of you. She wishes she could have the same type of relationship with me that you have with me."

"Poppa Pace, I know she doesn't like me, but Tasha and I were never close friends, so I'm not missing anything."

"The point is I don't want you to let Tasha's negative behavior towards you cause you to sin."

"What do you mean by that, Poppa Pace? Tasha is the one with the problem, not me." I pull into the parking lot at the diner, turn off the car engine, and face Poppa Pace. For a second, I wonder if she's already said anything to him about what she saw outside Alex's place.

"Daughter NikkiMac, I think some of the problem is with you. Tasha is not what she should be. The Lord knows I wish she would come back to the church and be faithful. She's not nice to you, and I see that. But it's pretty clear to me that you can't stand her either. Maybe it's because you feel protective of me, or because Tasha purposely tries to get under your skin. I grant you that most of the time, she's not easy to love. Yet, as members of the body of Christ, we are called to love our enemies. It pleases God when we have agape love for them; the kind of love that seeks their highest good. This doesn't come naturally to us. The Holy Spirit empowers us to love our enemies. Jesus tells us this in Matthew chapter 5, verses 43 through 48. It's a radical concept, that's for sure, but that's what the Lord commands. Sometimes, your enemy is in your own home, a family member. Tasha is my family, and I don't love her behavior, but I must love her. Of course, I use wisdom in dealing with her. She had to leave my house and I don't give her money, but I will give her food and I still pray for her. Pray about your attitude toward Tasha, and about anyone else who may be an enemy. You'll get divine help. You'll have peace about people who are otherwise unlovable. I want the best for you, Daughter NikkiMac."

I look into his caring eyes. They are the color of dark roast coffee. His sincere gaze makes me feel ashamed, then touched. Once again, Poppa Pace teaches me by word and example how to walk righteously, and he always gives credit to the Lord. "Poppa Pace, thank you for being both honest and compassionate with me. You're right about my attitude with Tasha, and she's not the only person I get funky with on a regular basis. Brother Darius has been trying to initiate a conversation with me for awhile, but I dismiss him. I remember the teaching in the scripture you mentioned, too. Why is it that I can sit in church service Sunday after Sunday as well as Bible study classes, and still not do what's right? Sometimes I get so frustrated with myself." I hit the steering wheel with the bottoms of my palms.

"Calm down, NikkiMac," he says mildly. "We are all a work in progress. Sanctification is a process. Pray and yield to the Spirit. Practice doing what God commands. It will be all right." We exit the car. He treats me to one of his comforting hugs.

Inside the diner, we get seated and busy ourselves with the menu. This place is always crowded on Sunday afternoons, but there's a quick turnover. The prices are reasonable, the food is delicious, and due to the large portions, most people leave carrying takeout containers of food. I enjoy diners because I can get breakfast, lunch, or dinner food at any time of the day. Poppa Pace orders the breakfast special with eggs, Canadian bacon, hash browns, and hot cakes. I choose the half portion of baked chicken, mixed veggies, and mashed potatoes. The server quickly brings coffee for Poppa Pace and water with lemon for me, then goes to the kitchen to place our food orders.

"Daughter NikkiMac, how are things at your job?"

"Teaching is tough, but it's rewarding. My students are important to me, and the classroom is never dull, but I do get tired of the excessive paperwork. I know some of it is necessary and helpful, but a lot of the forms, reports, standardized testing, and many versions of lesson planning can drive a teacher crazy! Sometimes I think the central administration tries to figure out how many ways they can make teachers accountable on paper. Meanwhile, so many disruptions eat into instructional time: managing behavior, completing paperwork, dealing with the social and emotional needs of numerous students. The intercom announcements regularly interrupt lessons; it makes me want to scream!" I feel myself getting warmed up.

"Your passion reveals that you have found your true life's work, NikkiMac." Poppa Pace smiles gently and pats my hands. He probably senses that I'm on a roll and need to vent; that's cool with me.

"A major concern is people who think our inner city children can't learn. It really ticks me off when staff members *show* that they don't like our children and treat them like they are substandard. Some teachers have low expectations and don't motivate or command the highest achievement from our students. These are the same teachers who, as soon as they can get out of the school building, haul-tail it out of Trenton. But, they don't have any trouble collecting those paychecks twice a month!"

"Daughter NikkiMac, it's a good thing that the Lord placed you and others like you in our schools. Our children need all the caring help they can get."

"I'm sorry, Poppa Pace. I don't mean to preach. Don't get me wrong, there are some truly dedicated teachers in our schools. All I ask is that teachers treat our students the way they want their own children to be treated by their teachers. And please don't let me get started about the parents who refuse to cooperate with us in the education of their children." I have to stop myself, because I can go on forever on this topic.

"Amen to that. Now, let's give thanks for the food we are about to receive." Poppa Pace prays for our food before it arrives, thanking God for it and asking God to bless it. This is a practice we adopted after our first meal together, when I started eating as soon as the food was placed in front of me. That day, Poppa Pace gently called my attention to it, and I felt like an embarrassed little pig.

After prayer, the food arrives. As our server places it before us, its aroma makes me salivate. I thank her without even looking up, because my fork is at the ready. I can't wait to feel and taste those mashed potatoes on my tongue.

"Excuse me, don't I know you? Is your name NikkiMac?" The server looks closely at my face. "Did you used to go to Club Taste a long time ago? I'm Mabel; I work in the kitchen there."

"Wow! Mabel, I haven't seen you in years! How have you been? How is Theo? What about Leisha and Nicole, do you still see them?"

"Theo is doing fine; he got a job working for the state, so he only tends bar on weekends now. Leisha and Nicole still come in the bar on weekends and prop their middle-aged bottoms on the barstools. One of them told me that you had started going to church. That's nice. All I knew for sure was that I never saw you back in Club Taste anymore. I'm doing fine, too. I'm the manager here, but I'm filling in for one of the servers today. Gotta do what I gotta do, you know?"

"I hear that. Mabel. Please meet Mr. Foster Pace. He's a member of the church. As a matter of fact, I actually met him the last night I was at Club Taste. He was walking through the parking lot at just the right time." I smile warmly at Poppa Pace.

"It's nice to meet you, Mr. Pace. Mabel Stone is my name."

"Hello, Ms. Stone, it's a pleasure to make your acquaintance. Do you attend church here in Trenton?" Poppa Pace never wastes an opportunity to evangelize. I need to be more like that.

"No, I don't. I haven't been to church in years, but I do watch some of the television preachers every now and then." Poppa Pace nods and wears a patient grin. I know he's planning the most effective evangelism approach for Mabel.

She looks at me closely. "NikkiMac, you heard about what happened to Darius Muse, right? He sure hit the wrong man's sister. Her brother heard about it, came to Trenton from Baltimore, and sliced Darius' arm so bad he had to have part of it amputated. He won't be hitting on another woman with that hand. This was about a year ago. Anyway, I'd better get back to work. It's good to see you. Hope to see you again soon." I wave goodbye, but I'm still processing what she said about Darius and his arm.

Poppa Pace gets her attention before she gets completely away. "Here you go, Mabel, take this tract and read it when you have a chance. It has wonderful information about the church. You are always welcome to join us in worship and Bible study." Poppa Pace hands her the same type of tract he gave me all those years ago. She smiles, thanks him, and goes to take another customer's food order.

Chapter 22 Brother Luke's Roller Skate Date

"Did you have a nice time at lunch with Brother Pace, NikkiMac?"

"Yes, Jacee, it was great. As usual, he gave me some wise advice about dealing with people, especially people who get on my nerves."

"I hear you, girl. I think most of us need help when it comes to that."

It's Sunday night, right after evening worship service. Jacee is in the kitchen of my house. I'm in the living room, in my recliner. We both have to work tomorrow, but decide to get together for a short while at my place. I live closer to the church building than does Jacee. My old house is almost the last one on a dead end street, near the old train freight yard. Occasionally, I hear a train whistle late at night. It's a noise that comforts me. The yard isn't near as active now, but long ago it was really busy. I know well the sounds of the train cars coupling and uncoupling, the grinding of the lumbering train wheels, and the lonesome polecat tenor of the whistle. These noises often lulled me to sleep when I was a child.

This is the house I grew up in. It used to be a row house, but over the years, Dad managed to buy the lots on either side. He had the houses leveled, made a carport on one side, and Mom cultivated a gorgeous garden on the other. Mom and Dad used to tell me the neighborhood was mostly working-class Polish and Italian when they moved in. I was born years after they purchased the home. As I grew up, the population changed. I guess it's the same as happens in all neighborhoods. The factories closed down or moved out of Trenton. Many of our former neighbors moved to other parts of the city, or to the townships. Others died, and their children chose not to stay here.

I need to be here; it comforts me to live here. I make renovations as I choose, but I keep some of my parents' touches. When I get good and ready, I'll buy another house and move into it. Tonight, I just chill while

Jacee busies herself in my kitchen, where she's fixing our tea. She's as familiar with this house as I am.

"NikkiMac, let me just tell you, Brother Lawrence Luke almost got on my last nerve." I sit up when I hear the bass in her voice.

"Jacee, come in here. Sit, take a sip of your ginger tea, and tell me all about it." She enters the room, hands me a cup, and sits in her favorite big chair.

"Remember when I first talked with you about Lawrence? We were at the diner that Sunday night."

"Of course I remember. He was sweating you really hard, and you hadn't been seeing him that long."

"NikkiMac, when Lawrence came back to church and showed an interest in me, I was quite pleased. You know how few eligible Christian men we meet, so I considered him to be a blessing. I figured we'd get to know one another, see if we could build a friendship. The male companionship was great at first, but certain behaviors of his seemed to have a mean or controlling edge. You and I discussed this, and then I spoke to him about my concerns. He said he'd try to comply with my wishes, because that's how much he wanted our relationship to grow."

"Has he changed the behaviors that concerned you, Jacee?"

"He did for a short time. Then, one day he got mad and let it slip that *you* were the reason he and I couldn't get closer."

"Me? He blamed me for his stupid behavior? Watch me laugh!"

"NikkiMac, just like you predicted, Lawrence popped the sex question, and I gave him the celibacy speech. Lawrence feels the reason I can't get close to him or any other man is because I am too attached to you. He actually said that you and I must be gay for each other, because we don't seem to want or need a man."

My laughter stops, and I feel heat rush up the back of my neck. "What about the fact that you, me, and many other single Christians are trying to get to heaven? That's why we aren't jumping on every Tom, Dick, and Harry, or Sally, Sue, and Holly in heat!" I'm getting fired up now. "Lawrence is so bogus. He needs to get down on his knees and pray. What if you were weak in the faith and had gotten yourself all caught up in his program? That situation would have been a hot mess!"

"Don't worry, NikkiMac, I got this. I didn't dignify his gay remarks with a response, but I told him our dating relationship was over. He said he'd place his church membership elsewhere if I stopped seeing him. Let's see Lawrence get a letter of recommendation from Minister Johnson, if he doesn't repent. He slandered me and you, and all along he had a plan to get in my panties. I'm sure going to tell Brother Johnson, because some other woman may fall for his facade and get hurt, or leave the church."

"Jacee, you're better off without him. I'm glad you didn't fall for the okey doke of a man who's a Christian in name only. I do have one question, though. What was up with lusty Lawrence and the late Sister Keke? He really performed at her funeral. Remember me telling you about that?"

"Yes I do, NikkiMac. I asked him about that, and he admitted to being a former client of the late Sister Keke. He said he stopped using her services long before he became a Christian, and once she became a Christian, she was kind enough to never bring it up. Girl, I didn't even want to know the extent of the services she provided to him." Jacee makes a comical face at me. I shake my head and grin.

"So, Brother Luke admits that he was skuzzy enough to use an escort service in the past, but thinks it's all right to call you gay because you refuse to fornicate with him. Sister Keke was a lot better than he is, God rest her soul. At least she allowed the Lord to change her life when she came to Christ. Brother Luke is in the church, but he's not in the kingdom of God, because he isn't following God's will. He's making false accusations about us, asking you for sex, and fronting that he's faithful. He's not looking out for others like Sister Keke did. Judging from the turnout of men at her funeral, she could have named lots of names while she was living, but she didn't."

"I know that's right, NikkiMac. Don't worry about me, I'll be just fine. I was fine before Brother Luke and I'll be fine now that I've given him his roller skate date."

"Roller skate date?"

"Yes, as in, put on your roller skates and skate on out of my life." We both laugh and finish our tea. Then, Jacee gathers her things and prepares to leave. At my front door, we do our familiar sisterly embrace.

"I think the best plan is for us is to focus on living faithfully, and not on looking for mates. If God wants us to have Christian husbands, God will provide the ones who are perfect for us. Our job is to follow His divine will. I'm proud of you, Jacee; you made the right decision about Lawrence. Part of what Brother Pace told me today was to forgive people who don't treat you correctly. Don't hold a grudge against Lawrence, and I'll also pray that I don't get an attitude because of his remark about us being gay for each other."

"I hear you, NikkiMac. Thanks for listening. Have a good night, my sister." I watch her walk down my front steps and get into her car. I finally close my front door when I see her drive away safely.

Chapter 23   We Don't See Eye to Eye

I am excited this Sunday morning! Alex called last night and said he would be attending the morning church service today. I haven't been in communication with him much lately, but that's not surprising. I've been keeping my distance due to a commitment to God to end fornication. I recognize that I have both a friendly closeness and a sexual attraction to Alex, so I need to back up until my sexual desire is under control. There's an old saying among some church folk about running toward trouble to prove how strong you are in the faith. It doesn't make sense to me. I've proven it to be wrong with Alex. Besides, the Bible says to run away from fornication; that's what I'm doing with my buddy Alex. He still doesn't agree with my decision, but says he's willing to listen to a sermon. He said he might even speak with Brother Johnson about the church. Our phone conversation last night was brief, but an air of conflict did surface.

"NikkiMac, I miss having you as my friend. We don't even talk on the phone anymore. You kicked a brother to the curb." His opening statement tugged at my heartstrings. I also miss our playful and easy banter.

"Alex, I miss you as my friend, too. You know what I am trying to do, though. I'm not avoiding you just to be mean. I'm making sure I don't have sex with you."

"You act like sex is the focus of our friendship, and that's definitely not the case."

"Alex, do I detect an attitude?" We both chuckled at my remark; it's one of our private jokes.

"NikkiMac, I'll meet you at church tomorrow morning. What time does morning service start?"

"Sunday School starts at 9:45."

"Whoa, hold up! I'm not trying to hear it all in one day! When is the main service?"

"It starts at 11:00. I'm glad you plan to attend, Alex."

"Maybe I can learn why you stress so much about an occasional bit of intimacy between good friends."

"I'm sure you'll benefit from attending our worship service. See you in the morning, Alex." After last night's phone conversation, I thanked God.

Now, we are about to begin service. Jacee arrives and takes her seat next to me. I wave to Cletus, who's sitting with some people a few pews away. As soon as I think it, Jacee says it. "That looks like Angeleese and her posse sitting next to Cletus. What's up with that, NikkiMac?"

"I'm sure I don't know about that, but get ready, because Alex called me last night and said he was coming to church this morning."

"Great balls of fire! It's going to be an interesting Sunday morning!" Jacee looks gleeful. She knows about the longstanding friendship I share with Alex, but I never told her about the sex. I didn't want to see the disappointment in her eyes that the revelation would cause. As far as she knows, Alex is my best male pal. I must have just talked him up, as the old folks say, because right now he's being led to this pew by Usher Dexter.

"Sister NikkiMac, this gentleman says he's a guest of yours. He'd like to sit with you."

"Yes, he is my guest. Thank you, Brother Dexter." I move so Alex can sit between Jacee and me. Both of us give him a warm handshake. He smiles confidently at me. I am happy he is here to learn about the gospel. I also like the smell of his cologne.

Brother Flowers opens service. "Brothers, sisters, visiting friends, it is time for us to begin our morning worship service. Are there any prayer requests?"

Sister Batts stands. I hear someone groan. "Brother Flowers, as you all know, I am Sister Batts." She pauses for effect and turns so all can see her and her outfit, then she continues. "I am very much involved in teaching a Bible class to the people on my job. This is because I want their souls to be saved. The Bible tells us in the Great Commission that we are to teach the good news to everyone, and that is what I strive to do. I take this charge very seriously. In my scholarly efforts, I…"

"Excuse me, Sister Batts; do you have a prayer request at this time?" Brother Flowers looks like he's trying really hard to be polite. I hear a few sighs.

"Yes, Brother Flowers, I do have a request. My boss has threatened to put a letter in my personnel file if I don't limit my Bible class to employee break times or lunch times. Please pray for me so I can be bold and press on for the Lord."

"Sister Batts, your request has been heard; it will be sent up in prayer. I will say this, though. Your employer hired you to do a job, and the Bible tells us we are to be good employees. Perhaps you will consider this, along with the request from your boss, about limiting your workplace teaching to the suggested times. Christians should be the best employees a boss has." Sounds of approval are heard. Sister Batts looks like she wants to rebut Brother Flowers' remarks, but she tightens her lips and sits down.

"Are there any other prayer requests?"

"I will be having surgery this coming Friday. Please pray that God will bless the doctors and staff in doing my procedure. Pray that I put my trust in God and not be afraid. Also, please pray for my recovery." Sister Longstreet speaks this in a soft and humble voice.

"Amen."

"God will be with you, my sister."

"Yes, Lord."

"Is there anyone else?" Brother Flowers surveys the auditorium. Cletus stands up, clears his throat, and then speaks.

"Church, I need prayer to help me make the right decisions about a situation that has shown up in my life. I need to do what the Lord tells me is right, not simply what is convenient for me. Please pray for me. Thank you." Next to Cletus, Angeleese and her children bow their heads and clasp their hands. It looks like they are praying.

"Amen, brother."

"Alright, brother."

I wonder if this has anything to do with Angeleese's claim that Cletus is the father of her twins. The thought prompts me to look in their direction again. Angeleese and her children are still in the prayer position, until Cletus taps Angeleese on her shoulder. She then raises her head and taps the child next to her. Like reverse falling dominoes; they all lift up their heads and unfold their hands. Jacee notices this too.

"I guess they all had their eyes closed, so they didn't hear or see Cletus stop talking and sit back down after his prayer request, huh?"

"Cut it out, Jacee, don't get me started."

Alex chimes in. "You ladies behave yourselves, please," he teases. He smiles at us in a friendly manner. Brother Flowers offers prayer for the requests. Brother Vincent starts off the singing with *Holy, Holy, Holy.* Alex seems familiar with this hymn. I enjoy his baritone voice. Brother Vincent leads us in two more hymns, and then Poppa Pace goes forward to lead the scripture reading. I notice him raise an eyebrow in curiosity as he sees Alex sitting between me and Jacee. I give him a reassuring wink.

"Today's scripture reading is found in First Corinthians chapter 10, verses 1 through 13." Poppa Pace pauses as we turn pages in our Bibles. Usher Gray brings a Bible to Alex. I help him find First Corinthians and notice he's aware it's in the New Testament section of the Bible. Folks unfamiliar with the Bible usually start from Genesis and flip the pages until they find the book they want. Others first turn to the page in the front of the Bible that lists the books and their page numbers; then turn to the selected text.

Alex appears to know more about the Bible than I thought. The surprise must show on my face, because he leans over and whispers, "What? You think your buddy Alex is a total heathen? I have had a Bible in my hands before, Missy."

Poppa Pace reads the scripture out loud; we follow along in our Bibles. Then, we bow our heads for prayer.

"Heavenly Father, thank you for bringing us here safely to worship you in spirit and in truth. Please add a blessing to the reading, hearing, and obeying of your word. Help us all consider this First Corinthians passage seriously. Keep us from chasing after what is evil. Help us lean on You in all our ways. Put it in our hearts to be cautious so we don't slip into sin. Make us remember that as children of God, whatever we go through, You are with us. You will make a way through the trouble if we put our trust in You. Father, please touch the hearts of those in this audience who have not been added to the body of Christ. Encourage them to answer the gospel call today. All this we pray in the name of our Lord and Savior, Jesus Christ. Let the church say…"

The church says, "Amen." So does Alex. Angeleese and her children say it several times before Cletus gently shushes them. They don't seem to mind this; they get quiet.

After Brother Vincent leads us in *Yield Not To Temptation* and *Take My Life, And Let It Be*, five brothers come forward to lead communion. Alex asks me if he should take communion, even though he's not a member of the church. I shake my head to indicate that he shouldn't. He looks relieved. Maybe he thinks the unleavened bread and the fruit of the vine will make him melt. All goes well, except when the communion trays get near Scooter and Ziggy, Angeleese's oldest children. They are sitting the farthest away from her on the pew. Before she or Cletus can stop them, they each grab one of the small communion cups. They proceed to throw back their heads, gulp the grape juice, smack their little lips, and loudly say, "Ahh." They sound like miniature winos. One of the servers deftly takes the communion cups from them and replaces them in the tray. Angeleese looks puzzled. Cletus looks embarrassed. People who understand children smile; those who don't frown. When communion is over, we sing *Heavenly Sunlight* and *No, Not One*. Minister Johnson comes to the pulpit to preach.

"Good morning. I'm happy to see you all this fine Sunday morning. I trust that you have come to worship in spirit and in truth. Before I begin the message, let me welcome our visitors. You are always welcome; we consider you our honored guests. Our hope and prayer is that you respond to the gospel call and put on Jesus Christ in baptism for the remission of your sins. Christ will add you to His church, and you will receive the gift of the Holy Spirit, who will guide you in righteousness. Live faithfully, and when Jesus returns to claim those that are His, you will live with Him in heaven for eternity. There, I pretty much just preached all one needs to know to be added the church. Is there anyone here who is ready to confess that Jesus Christ is the Son of God? Is there anyone here who wants to repent of their sins? Is there one who wants to be added to the church right now? You don't have to wait for me to complete today's sermon." Brother Johnson pauses and looks over the congregation.

Alex whispers, "That sure is a mouthful!"

I elbow him softly. "Now who's misbehaving?"

"I thank all the brothers who have served in our worship thus far in leading songs and prayer and reading the scripture. Brother Pace did a fine job reading our focus scripture for this morning from the first 13 verses of First Corinthians chapter 10. When he offered prayer, he almost stole my sermon for the day!"

"That's right, Brother Johnson!'

"Amen!"

Poppa Pace smiles and exclaims, "Excuse me, Brother Johnson. I didn't mean to steal your thunder!"

"No, no. It's all good, Brother Pace. Whenever the word of truth is proclaimed, it's all right! Maybe somebody was receptive to the prayer you offered and is deciding right now. Perhaps after the sermon, they will make that decision to come to the Lord."

"Say so, preacher!'

"Praise the Lord!"

"This morning, I'm going to give you the title for the sermon right at the beginning. You know that once I get started, I often forget to do so. This gives the brother doing the tape and CD ministry a fit, because he can't properly label the cassettes and CDs for you." We see the brother in the recording booth smile broadly and give a thumbs-up gesture from behind the glass.

"The title of today's sermon is *Look for the Way Out*. Some of you may think that's an unusual sermon title, but consider today's Bible passage First Corinthians chapter 10." The sounds of pages turning, a few babies' noises, and someone's cell phone are heard.

"Through the help of the Holy Spirit, I plan to walk down your street today with this sermon, but I am coming to you in love and with concern for your souls. Sometimes, after I preach a sermon, a person will say that it felt like I was talking directly to them without calling their name. A person will ask how I know about their particular sin. I assure you that I don't spy on Christians. I do not listen to gossip about church members. God doesn't call me to do that. He calls me to preach the gospel. God knows about our sins. He is omniscient, so He knows all. He is omnipresent, so He's everywhere. He is also omnipotent, so He's all powerful. The Bible tells us that Jesus, the Son of God, was on this earth in human form. He was tempted like we are tempted. He was tempted in *all* the ways we are tempted to sin, but Jesus did *not* sin! Look at Hebrews chapter 4, verses 15 through 16. We see here that we can get divine help to overcome our temptations. When you get to thinking that Christ can't identify with what you're going through and can't aid you, look at Hebrews chapter 2, verse 18. Saints, can you hear me out there?" Brother Johnson cups his hand to one ear and waits for audience response.

"Thank you, Jesus!"

"Amen, brother!"

"Preach it!"

"Christians, that is why we need to look for the way out of our temptations. God has provided an escape plan. The Bible gives us direction. We have to pray, look for the way out, and take the escape plan before we are drawn to the temptation and succumb to it. Say 'Amen' when you can!"

"Amen, preacher!"

"That's all right, brother!"

"In this message, I'm going to offer a small number of scenarios where we can scripturally apply the sermon title: *Look for the Way Out*. Think biblically about how to handle temptation. Let the scriptures speak when we need to look for a way out. Is that all right, church?"

"Go ahead, brother!"

"Preach, brother!"

"Fasten your seatbelts, because here we go!

"Come on, brother!"

"Tell it!"

"Someone offers you a business deal that would profit you enormously, and you are tempted to jump at this opportunity. You investigate and find out that this deal will financially benefit you, but it's not completely legal. Chances are high that no one will find out about it, and you'll walk away with thousands of dollars in profit. The temptation to put financial profit before honesty stares you in the face. Look for the way out. God sees everything, and He tells us to be honest in our dealings with others. Write these scriptures in your notes for personal Bible study: First Peter chapter 2, verse 12; Romans chapter 12, verse 17; Second Corinthians chapter 13, verse 7. Write it down, write it down!"

"Amen, preacher!"

"That's all right!"

"You're out at dinner with colleagues and the conversation turns negative about a difficult coworker who isn't present. You admire these colleagues and know they can help your career. You purposely avoid comment, but someone in the group asks your opinion of the absent colleague. The temptation to get ahead by putting someone else down stares you in the face. Look for the way out. Write these scriptures in your notes: James chapter 1, verse 26 and chapter 3, verse 5; First Peter chapter 3, verse 10. I'm giving you plenty of holy homework today, my friends."

"It's alright, brother!"

"That's what the book says!"

"You are often excluded from party gatherings of your associates because people know you are a Christian who doesn't drink alcoholic beverages, use profanity, gossip, or enjoy vulgar jokes. Instead, when you are invited, you use every opportunity to invite others to church and share the gospel. You are sometimes discouraged and wish you were better received by these associates in their social settings. The temptation to be a part of the crowd stares you in the face. Look for the way out. The first of the Psalms, in verse 1, tells us about the kind of company we shouldn't allow to influence us. First Corinthians chapter 15, verse 33 cautions us about our associates."

"That's right!"

"Amen! Amen!"

"In order to get that great job promotion, you must agree to work on Sundays. This means you will regularly miss both morning and evening Sunday worship services. The temptation to put your job before attending worship services stares you in the face. Say it with me!"

"Look for the way out!" Our voices are so loud that they almost overpower Brother Johnson's voice.

"Hallelujah! In Hebrews chapter 10, verses 24 through 25, we are instructed to be faithful in worship as well as told why we need to do so."

"Say so, preacher!"

"Good point!"

"God will make a way, preacher!"

"Sister Yes and Brother No are two Christians who get on your last nerve. They are backwards and have poor hygiene. You are ashamed to have them around your other friends. The temptation to avoid them stares you in the face. You know where I'm going with this, church. You need divine help to adjust your attitude. Sometimes, *you* are the source of your problem. What should you do?"

A loud chorus of "Look for the way out!" rises to the church ceiling. I even notice a response from one of the teenagers who's usually texting on the sly.

"You feel the need for companionship, so you date. At some point, mutual sexual desire surfaces. The temptation to act on that desire stares you in the face. Look for the way out. You know what God says about fornication and adultery. Yes, I said adultery. Unfortunately, there are some spouses who are lonely in marriage and seek outside companionship, but I'll get to that in another sermon on marriage. Let me focus here on those who are unmarried. From the beginning, God set a design for human sexuality. In Genesis chapter 1, verses 26 through 28, we read that God created male and female. He introduced sexuality in the union of Adam and Eve. In Genesis chapter 2, verses 18 through 25, we read how God made woman from man's rib and declared they were for each other as man and wife. In a marriage union, sexuality intimacy is blessed. Male and female, husband and wife; that's God's design. I know I may not get many affirmations for this particular point, but God's word is true."

I say, "Amen."

Jacee says, "Amen."

Many members of the church say, "Amen."

Alex says nothing.

Brother Johnson ends the sermon. With outstretched arms, he offers the call to baptism. Brother Vincent faces the congregation and starts the invitation song, *When The Roll Is Called Up Yonder*. Alex stands rigidly between me and Jacee. He does not even try to sing, even though I hand him a songbook that's turned to the correct page. I strain my peripheral vision and see that his expression says, "I am truly not feeling this!" I'm initially disappointed, because I really want him to accept Christ today. Then, I remember that many people refuse to accept Christ after hearing only one sermon, or being in one Bible study. People usually have a hard time letting go of their own way in order to embrace God's will. It also takes an honest heart to respond to Jesus. At the end of the last verse, Brother Johnson reminds all that it's not too late to respond. He waits for a bit, and no one accepts the gospel call, so he gestures for us to be seated.

The ushers start collecting the offering while Brother Vincent leads another hymn. Although I tell Alex he doesn't have to contribute because he's not a member of the church, he still tosses a couple of dollars in the collection basket.

Brother Martin begins the announcements next. "Please refer to your church bulletins, especially the sick and shut in list. Remember Sister Retha, who hasn't been able to come out to services for two Sundays. She has a serious respiratory infection. Brother Kelsey is in Mercy Hospital; he can have visitors. Our brother is way up there in years and he's still faithful. Please pray for and visit him; we know he'd be here if he could."

"Amen, brother."

"Also, the young people who are going to the Youth Conference at our sister congregation in Newark must be at the building next Saturday by 8:45 in the morning. This alert is for the parents, because we know you are the ones who have to bring your children here. Remember, we adults have to be on time in order to teach children the importance of timeliness. We need to arrive in Newark for the early registration session, so any stragglers will be left behind. I will be driving the church van and Lord willing, that church van will be pulling out of here at 9:00 in the morning, not at 9:05, not at 9:06, not at 9:07, and so on." Brother Martin pauses and looks over the audience. His expression is pleasant, but serious. I fully expect him to launch into his speech about people not being grateful enough for free transportation to show up on time for it. Some others must be thinking the same thing, so they attempt to avert the familiar speech by responding to him.

"That's right, Brother Martin!"

"Amen."

"Say so, Brother Martin!"

We successfully dodge an announcement bullet, because Brother Martin quickly wraps up the announcements and we stand for closing prayer. Afterwards, Jacee says goodbye to Alex. She gives me a quick hug; she's going to meet her parents for a family meal. I turn to Alex. "Thank you for coming to service today, Alex. It means a lot to me."

"You're welcome, NikkiMac. Actually, I'm glad I attended, because your preacher's sermon settled something in my mind about our friendship." I feel butterfly wing excitement. Does Alex finally understand why our friendship had to change? Does he realize we can still be good buddies, only without sex, like before? Suddenly, a force knocks into the back of my legs and I almost topple into Alex's arms.

"Sasha, you stop running around in church! Grab her, Sister NikkiMac, please!" Sister Coles' plaintive cry jars me back. I grab the chunky little dynamo by the arms and hold her. Her head, with its many colorful barrettes bangs against me as she squirms and giggles. I hand her off to Sister Coles and turn around to address Alex, but he's no longer in the auditorium. I quickly speak to a few people, and then go to the lobby to look for Alex. I notice Poppa Pace first. He must see something significant in my facial expression, because he shifts direction and starts walking to me. All of a sudden, a firm hand grabs mine from behind. It's Alex.

"Alex, I thought you'd left! What happened? Why did you walk away like that without saying anything to me?"

"Relax NikkiMac. I had to use the men's facilities. I do have something to say to you before I leave, though."

"Do you want to talk here, or do you want to speak with Minister Johnson? Perhaps you have some questions about the sermon, or about how to become a Christian?" I realize I sound desperate, but I can't stop babbling. Alex guides me back into the auditorium; no one else is in there but us. Alex has a stern expression as he speaks.

"NikkiMac, today is the last day we are going to interact with one another. It's for the best."

I try hard not to look like a deer caught in the headlights. "Why? What are you saying, Alex?"

"You know how crazy I am about our friendship; we've been buddies for so many years. I heard what your minister said today about sexual intimacy being acceptable only in marriage, but I just don't see it that way."

When Alex agreed to attend worship service, I had such hope that he would really hear the gospel, understand where I'm coming from, and that we could resume our pre-sexual friendship. Now I begin to feel that hope fade. "Alex, our minister and all of us read those verses from the Bible. Brother Johnson wasn't giving you his opinion; he told us what

God says in the scriptures." I am having trouble with Alex not getting this. He is definitely an intelligent man.

"You've said the same things to me, NikkiMac. Did you think I would better accept them if I heard them from the pulpit? NikkiMac, organized religion simply is not my thing. I feel like I'm a pretty nice guy. I give to charity and try to treat people fairly. I've told you before that I believe in God. I just don't think I need to come to church in order to show my love for Him. I also believe that God created men and women for each other, and that the intimacy shared by two consenting adults is beautiful. The two of us escalated from friends, to friends with a physical relationship. I thought it was a wonderful escalation. NikkiMac, once you gave that intimacy to me, it was wrong for you to take it back. Here's the thing: I respect you and our friendship too much to let this issue make us bitter with each other. You have attempted to exercise restraint in our relationship. Obviously, I don't agree that it's needed, but I give you credit for trying to do what you believe is right. However, I am always going to enjoy your company as well as desire you in a physical way. Since we can't get together anymore without this temptation, let's end this now. That way, we'll always have fond, sweet memories of a lovely friendship. Goodbye, my buddy." Before I can open my mouth, he leans over and kisses me on my forehead. Then, he walks out of the auditorium.

Several emotions quickly slam inside me. I go from feeling indignant, to feeling betrayed, to feeling the lightening of a burden, to feeling abandoned, to feeling like a door is opening, to feeling sad. All this sensation floods over me in a minute, it seems. Then, from far away in my mind, I sense the doors of the auditorium open and close softly. Someone's here.

"Daughter NikkiMac, are you all right? I saw your guest leave. Don't feel bad. Some people need lots of sermons and Bible studies before they get baptized. At least you encouraged him to come to a church service. He got a chance to hear the gospel. It's up to him to decide; you've done your part." Poppa Pace faces me and puts his arm around my stiff shoulders. After taking a deep breath, I confess.

"That's the problem, Poppa Pace. I did my part, but only after I'd set the wrong example."

"Go on, you know you can tell me anything you need to."

"His name is Alex. I have been friends with him for the longest time, but at one point, our friendship became sexually intimate. After a while, I became convicted of this sin, so I repented and asked God for forgiveness. I also asked Alex to forgive me because I'd sinned with him. He looked at me like I was crazy. I even stopped contact with him, so I wouldn't dance in the way of temptation. When he finally did call and ask me about church, I was so hopeful that he would hear and obey the gospel of Christ. Poppa Pace, I am ashamed to tell you all this, but it's the truth." I feel lower than a snake's belly, and fight back tears.

"Daughter NikkiMac, calm yourself. You repented of your sin, asked God to forgive you, and tried to show Alex the right way. Why should you feel ashamed?"

"I'm ashamed because I was weak. I'm ashamed because you think so highly of me and that means so much to me. I let you down."

"Dear child, be more concerned about what God thinks of you. I am proud of you because you repented. Don't beat yourself up. Instead, forgive yourself the way God forgave you. About Alex, at least he heard the gospel today. Also, consider that God sometimes moves people out of His children's way in order to help them overcome sin. Think about today's scripture reading, First Corinthians chapter 10, verses 1 through 13." I stay quiet for a time and think about myself in reference to those scriptures. After that, I look up into the warm eyes of Poppa Pace.

"You know, you're right. God knows about my temptation with Alex, and He knows I want to obey Him. God has provided a way out for me with this situation. My task is to *take* that way."

"There you go, Daughter NikkiMac! God is good."

"And He's always right on time!" I feel my usual good humor trickling back. It actually feels better to have admitted this to Poppa Pace. I probably need to share this with Jacee; it might encourage her. It can remind her that no matter how strong we think we are, when we take our eyes off God, we fall into sin.

"Give me a hug, daughter. I've got to check the back doors." We embrace, and then Poppa Pace goes about his church business. On my way out of the church building, I wave at a few members. By the time I get outside, I no longer feel stunned and stung, but thoughtful and hopeful. This time, I notice Tasha do her herky-jerk walk up to me.

"Hey, Miss NikkiMac! What's up? See, I didn't sneak up on you like last time because you threatened me with bodily harm. Come to think of it, that wasn't very Christian of you, now was it?" Before opening my mouth, I pause and think about the fact that just like God made me, God also made Tasha. She's not His obedient child, but she is His child.

"Good afternoon, Tasha. Thank you for not startling me this time. Yes, you are correct; it was not very Christ-like for me to threaten you before. I apologize. Will you please accept my apology?" I don't know what surprises me more, the fact that I am reacting to Tasha this way, or that I genuinely feel what I am saying. This has got to be the work of the Holy Spirit, because it certainly isn't the work of NikkiMac.

For a moment, Tasha is silent. Next, both of her eyes uncharacter-istically focus on me, and one eyebrow lifts at the outer corner. Her expression says, "I'm going to see how much you mean this, NikkiMac. I'm going to push you a little further." She walks closer, violates my personal space and hisses, "No, I don't think I *will* accept your apology, Miss NikkiMac. What do you think about that, you fake Holy Girl?"

She's close enough that I can smell what she had for breakfast; it's not a friendly aroma. However, there's something going on within me that has my attention as I respond. "Tasha, I'm disappointed you don't want to accept the apology, but I said it and I meant it." I manage a smile that feels genuine.

"Well, I'm saying and meaning this. I saw you had your lover come to church today. Did you introduce him to my daddy? Did you tell my daddy that your visitor has been hitting your drawers? What, you think it's okay to get busy with Alex if he comes to church? Even I know that doesn't excuse sin, and I'm a sinner. Know this; I do plan to tell my daddy about your whoring ways. Soon and very soon, I plan to tell it!"

The Holy Spirit settles me, so I softly respond, "Tasha, I don't have to tell you this, but I will. There is nothing improper going on with me and Alex or me and any other man, or woman, for that matter. If you feel you must tell your father, my Poppa Pace, something about me, I can't do anything about that. You have to do what you have to do. My responsibility is to wish you well and pray for you. I have to go now. You have a very nice day."

I do not bother to watch her reaction. I get in my car, start it, and drive out of the parking lot. The sweet, encouraging melody and words of *Yield Not To Temptation* resonate in my head.

Chapter 24   Onward and Upward

We are nearing the end of our annual Church Children's Spotlight Program. This event gives our children the opportunity to show their knowledge of scripture through recitation, church songs, art projects, and skits with Bible themes. The program has been great thus far. I like that the children get positive reinforcement and encouragement from the adults here. It's not always easy being a church kid in today's society. If we don't support our children, other negative influences will more easily trap them. Brother Vincent puts his heart into the young men's training program. Jacee teams with me to work with the girls' classes. All of the children join together in the singing program that's directed by Brother Vincent. During today's program, the young men have led us in prayer. The children have created posters which are on display. They are full of positive messages for youth, and encouraging slogans abound:

"Jesus loves you, so be good!"

"Have you read your Bible today?"

"Do your best, and God will do the rest!"

"Your body is your temple, don't pollute it. Stay away from drugs!"

"Let only sweet words come from your mouth!"

"Stay out of trouble. Let God fight your battles for you!"

Some of these children, like Bobby and Antron, are quite artistic. I am extremely gratified, because the children are so joyful and proud of what they've prepared for this program. Also, many parents are here. It's a true saying that if you want lots of parent participation, give every child a part in the program. They usually show up to watch their children perform.

Shaylonda and Chastity now come before the audience. "We are going to recite Psalm 103 for you." Shaylonda starts with the first verse. Chastity recites the second verse. The girls continue taking turns as they flawlessly deliver the twenty-two verses. Then, they both curtsy with a flourish while we vigorously applaud them.

"They are just too much! Who told them to curtsy at the end of the recitation?" Jacee asks, but she smiles brightly as we clap in appreciation.

"Girl, you know Miss Shaylonda always has to put her flavor on everything she does!" I shake my head, laugh softly, and clap loudly. I'd rather see her here, proud of the fact that she can quote scripture from memory, instead of being in the nearby schoolyard shaking her behind.

"Thank you, Shaylonda and Chastity. You two young ladies did a fine job." Brother Vincent continues, "Church, I'm going to ask all of the children to come forward for a final bow. They did an excellent job tonight. They will each be rewarded with a certificate of recognition and a Church Children's Spotlight trophy. Thank you for coming out to celebrate our children. Continue to be Christian examples for them and pray for them. Please show them your appreciation with a major round of applause." We give our children a standing ovation. Every one of them wears a beaming smile, from Antron, who delivered a brief sermon about David and Goliath, to little Sasha Coles, who screamed out, "Jesus wep!" for her memory verse. It was supposed to be John chapter 11, verse 35, but Sasha hasn't quite mastered the final *t* consonant sound.

Brother Johnson comes to the microphone. "Brothers and sisters, I am floored by the fine Christian performances of our young people today! Congratulations to our parents and church teachers for diligently working with our youth. Let's recognize Brother Vincent, Sister NikkiMac, and Sister Jacee, because they are doing a marvelous job with our children!" As the audience stands and claps heartily for us, I feel a little embarrassed. I enjoy working with children, but for some reason, I feel uncomfortable with public recognition for doing do. Not Jacee, though. She bows, and then gives our audience the pleasure of viewing her thirty-two teeth. Brother Vincent nods politely at the crowd and claps for me and Jacee.

"There's a reception in our dining hall, please come and have light refreshments before you leave. And please, speak to and congratulate as many of our children by name as you can. It means a lot to them." Brother Johnson leads us in a prayer to close out the program and give thanks for the food. I notice teenager Bobby warmly embrace a boy I haven't seen here before. I want to congratulate Bobby for his extra help with the program. He's quite creative.

"Bobby, thank you again for all your work with the props; you certainly helped me out."

"You're welcome, Sister NikkiMac, glad to do it. I want you to meet Justice." He points to the young man next to him.

"Hello, Justice. It's nice to meet you. Is this your first visit to the church?"

"Yes, M'am, I just came to Trenton this week. I'm from Virginia."

"I am glad you came to the church program, Justice. Please come again for worship." I look closely at the two of them. "You know, I see a physical resemblance, are you two boys related? You look like you could be first cousins."

Bobby says in a matter of fact way, "Justice is my brother from another mother." I bat my eyelashes a couple of times before recovering from both what Bobby said, and the casual way he said it. "We have the same father, but we have different mothers. We're both thirteen, though." Bobby and Justice seem unfazed by these facts.

I recover and smile. "I'm glad you two are able to be together. Family is important." They both shake my hand and join some of the other children.

I think of a similar situation that happened to me during parent-teacher conferences at work. I was reviewing a student's report card with her mother when another student and mother entered the room. They all greeted each other in a friendly fashion. Then, the mothers informed me that the father of the two girls was parking the car.

"Miss McQuaige, he be up here in a minute and you can talk to him 'bout both his girls, 'cause he both of they baby daddy." I often tell Jacee that with the way men are making babies with so many different women, some of these children are going to end up procreating with or marrying their own kinfolk. What a mess this world is in today, all because people want to do their own thing and ignore what God says. We all better get it together before Jesus returns. I know that much.

I gaze at the children. Justice, Bobby, Shaylonda, Sasha, and the rest of the children talk, laugh, munch on cupcakes, chips and dip. They joyfully drink the juice that Jacee pours into colorful plastic cups. Fortunately, my best friend seems at peace these post-Lawrence Luke days. I haven't seen him for a few months; neither has Jacee.

"Yo! NikkiMac, I see that far away look in your eyes. Stop daydreaming and bring me some more of this Happy Farms juice, please. I'm running out and these are some thirsty children!" Jacee winks at me and resumes pouring juice.

"No, Jacee. No more juice; they've guzzled eight or ten cartons already. Sister NikkiMac is breaking out the bottles of water. Enough sugar for one session." Some of the children moan, but most of the parents cheer. I don't blame them for not wanting to deal with sugared-up children the rest of the day. Water is better for them anyway.

"I know that's right!" Brother Vincent agrees with my refreshment assessment and goes to get a case of the more environmentally-friendly bottles of water. Jacee laughs good-naturedly. Like me, she's still single. Like me, she's serene.

My thoughts turn inward. I know I am turning my own corners. Everyone is. I am not the best Christian I can be. I realize that I am a work in progress. I still have my reservations about Darius Muse and his sincerity in the church. I acknowledge that it's not my place to judge his motives. It is my place to encourage him as my brother in Christ. Maybe I'll shake his remaining hand (there I go again) next week and initiate some supportive conversation. I know it's a baby step, but it's a beginning.

Some nights find me very horny in my always-alone bed. I wish I had never had sex, especially pleasurable sex, like I had with Alex. A fantastic orgasm has always made me feel so, so effervescent! However, the guilt that follows fornication overshadows the effervescence. If I had never become sexually active, I wouldn't know what I'm missing, now that celibacy is my consistent practice. My current best strategy for dealing with this desire is prayer and physical exercise. I keep in mind that First Corinthians chapter 6, verses 19 through 20 tell me that my body is the temple of the Holy Spirit. I cannot in good conscience do whatever I choose with it. The same principal is true for feeding my body properly, watching my weight, and getting exercise. It's going to be alright, because God knows what I need. If it's His desire, He'll provide the right husband for me. If it's not in His plan for me, God will continue to show me how to be a faithful, content, single Christian woman. I plan to yield to God's will.

One of the younger members here cracks me up when he says, "If being a single virgin is the only way I can get to heaven, then I'll gladly go to heaven a virgin and single." I like his spirit.

It may be time to put some effort into forming an active fellowship group for the single and widowed members at this congregation. Brother Adam Greene might be the one to lead such a group. The unmarried men are outnumbered by the unmarried women here, but brothers like Carlos, Vincent, Darius, Cletus, Brother Elton, and Brother Cliff might be interested. The aim of the group would not be matchmaking, but more of sharing ideas about living faithfully as Christians without mates. Because I believe Hebrews chapter 13, verse 5, I know that Jesus is always with His children regardless of their marital status and that we are never alone. Perhaps some of the stronger members can support those who are struggling because they have just come out of worldly relationships. Anyway, it's worth discussing the idea with our minister. I'm gong to put that on my list of things to do.

The Lord continues to work on my quick tongue and critical attitude, but I need to yield to the Holy Spirit even more in this area of my life. That way, I can see more of the good in Usher Gray and respond to him in Christian love, even when he tries to annoy me. That's going to be a challenge, because I so enjoy getting back at him. He always looks like such a doofus when I retaliate, but when I do that, I'm acting just as ugly as he acts. Maybe God puts people like Usher Gray, Mad Maggie, Sister Batts, and Tasha in my path to help me gain a more Christ-like attitude.

I plan to start discussing spiritual matters again with my coworkers. I might be that Christian they meet who can influence them for Christ. If I care about someone's soul, I should tell them about salvation. I don't have to hit them over the head with the gospel, but I don't need to clam up because I assume they aren't interested. My lifestyle should show that by grace, I live for Jesus Christ.

I plan to count my blessings more. I have life. I am in the body of Christ. I have pretty good health, lively students, a steady paycheck, a home, transportation, and some distant relatives that I plan to get to know better. Jacee, my Christian family, and certainly Poppa Pace, are strong blessings. One of the hymns we sing during worship encourages us to name and count our blessings, and I just may do that. I mean really, get a sheet of poster board and a marker, and start writing and numbering them. Then, put it up in my bedroom, so the list of blessings is in my face when I awaken each day. It could increase my gratefulness and help me be a blessing to others.

Suddenly, one of the third grade students hollers plaintively in my direction. "Sister NikkiMac, can you get Sasha? She keeps putting her messy hands on our posters!" Little Sasha, free from Sister Coles, is marching near the posters with her icing-covered fat fingers. She's trying to swipe at the artwork. Two other children join in the complaint.

"No, Sasha! Stop it!"

"Somebody get her, please!"

Just before Sasha plants her soiled hands on a poster, I scoop her up into my arms. She giggles gleefully. "Thank you, Sister NikkiMac!" The three children relax and return to their chattering.

"Jacee, I'll be right back. I'm going to find Sister Coles and give Sasha to her."

"Hurry back, NikkiMac. Refreshment time is almost over and you're up next for trophy presentation duty. The children are excited about receiving those Church Children's Spotlight trophies from you."

"Chillax, my dear sister. I got you. This won't take long." I look around the building for Sister Coles. Sasha sings and laughs, even though she's been captured. I think she likes me. I find Sister Coles in the restroom. She's texting on her phone.

"Here's your little package, Sister Coles." My tone is not the friendliest. Sasha sings the chorus of *Yes, Jesus Loves Me*. I put her down. She claps her hands and stomps her feet to accompany herself in song.

"I thought she was with her daddy, Sister NikkiMac. Thank you for looking out for my little escape artist." She smiles at me and takes her child by the hand. I don't smile back at the younger woman. Sasha begins to cry.

"She's a regular Houdini, that's for sure, Sister Coles." Before I check myself, or let the Holy Spirit do it, I let go with, "You'd be surprised at how many parents lose their children forever because they don't keep a close eye on them. I know there are a lot of Christians around, but our church doors are open to the public. Anyone can enter. In the blink of an eye, Sasha could go missing. Here you are in the bathroom texting on your phone, while this child is running around loose and getting on the other children's nerves. You ought to be more careful about letting her get away from you."

Sister Coles stays quiet. She looks wounded. She slowly lifts Sasha and rests the child on her hip. I almost immediately realize that it wasn't so much what I said just then; it was the way I said it. I brought Sasha to her mother, but I also brought the wrong attitude. Now, I feel like two cents. Sister Coles may be a dizzy parent, but she is not a bad person. I feel like I just broke her down.

"Sister Coles, I am so sorry, I didn't mean to hurt your feelings. I won't knowingly do that again. Please accept my apology." I instinctively reach out to hug her and Sasha. Thank God, she accepts my gesture of repentance. I hug her, she hugs me back, and we both hug Sasha.

"Are we alright with each other, Sister Coles?"

"We're alright, Sister NikkiMac. I accept your apology and advice. What you said was true. It just kind of hurt to hear you say it like you did. But thanks for being real with me, instead of talking about me behind my back."

"Thank you for your forgiveness, Sister Coles."

"Thank you for asking for my forgiveness, Sister NikkiMac."

"Wanna be down, Mommy!" Sasha is antsy and ready to move. Sister Coles lowers Sasha and exits the restroom. Her hand firmly clasps one of her baby girl's. With her free hand, Sasha waves at me and yells, "Bye, bye, NeeMac!"

I follow them from the restroom, but stop after a few steps. My thoughts steal attention from my next task. I feel remorseful about my fast tongue and snarky attitude. I'm thankful Sister Coles accepted my apology, and I offer God a silent prayer for His forgiveness. I aim to do what's right, but sometimes I don't measure up. I've got to believe that I'll grow stronger as I stay in the church, study the Bible, and follow Christ. Verse 13 of Philippians chapter 4 lets me know that in Jesus' strength, I can overcome anything. I may continue to struggle with sin, but I will *not* leave the Lord's church, because in Christ is where I'll gain the victory.

Suddenly, I hear Jacee's loud voice. She's calling me. "Sister NikkiMac! Where are you? It's trophy time! The children are seated, but they're getting restless!"

I've got to skit, scat, and skedaddle. Duty calls.

Breinigsville, PA USA
31 January 2010
231591BV00001B/3/P